Denis Ever After

Also by Tony Abbott

The Summer of Owen Todd

The Copernicus Legacy series

The Secrets of Droon series

Lunch-Box Dream

The Postcard

Firegirl

TONY ABBOTT

Denis
Ever After

KATHERINE TEGEN BOOKS
An Imprint of HarperCollins Publishers

Katherine Tegen Books is an imprint of HarperCollins Publishers.

Denis Ever After
Text copyright © 2018 by Tony Abbott
Interior illustrations by Oamul Lu

Library of Congress Control Number: 2017951444
ISBN 978-0-06-249122-0

Typography by Torborg Davern
18 19 20 21 22   PC/LSCH   10 9 8 7 6 5 4 3 2 1
❖
First Edition

TO MY SISTERS
ARLENE AND BEATRICE
APRIL 30 1958–MAY 2 1958

I

HEAVEN OR WHATEVER

So this morning I'm taking a slow glide with GeeGee down to the shore and she tells me right out of the blue how it's almost five years since I died. GeeGee is my great-grandmother, and she says it like it's nothing.

"Five years."

We pause on the sidewalk. "Really? Five whole years?"

"Russell told me."

Russell is GeeGee's friend. Russell isn't magical or anything. He just writes stuff down.

"Thanks," I tell her. "I guess I forgot."

"Oh, Matt! A joke this early in the day!"

I'm not Matt. I'm Denis, Matt's twin brother. Matt is alive and twelve now. I'm one of those, but not both.

GeeGee tugs my arm when I correct her. "Denis, of course." We cross Water Street and start into the gently winding route to the harbor. "You begin losing it right away, don't you?" she says. "Your memory. I believe I'm around twenty-nine now."

She's not. She's over eighty. Maybe near ninety. GeeGee died when Matt and I were tiny, and she sometimes confuses me with him. Which is funny because people did that all the time when I was alive.

I drown and float and drown and float.

I love GeeGee; she's taught me so much about life and about being up here, but I think she's slipping away big-time, forgetting things more quickly than ever, which, believe it or not, is what you're supposed to do when you get to Port Haven.

I shiver among the yellow leaves.

For the last five years I've been on the road to becoming clean, too. Being clean is the total point when you die. You clear your life out of your system like, well, your food when you have a stomach bug. You shake off the heaviness, you become air.

I have a handful of memories of my family. My mom's smile, her wavy brown hair; her not hugging me so much, but my feeling warm and soft when she did. Dad was quiet as a stump in the morning, then told off-the-wall jokes at supper, like he was two different people. Maybe it was the afternoon beers he drank, but whatever. He taught me how to bike and play ball and other stuff. Mostly, I remember my brother, Matt, who I've known longer than anyone, because, obviously, we were born together.

GeeGee did get it right about forgetting. From the second we enter Port Haven, we start forgetting our lives. We do it in reverse, from the last moment we breathed real air to the very beginning, until basically we become unborn.

From the dark, the darker darkness rises.

And there is silver.

Naturally, *where* and *when* and *how* we died are the first things we forget. This is probably a good thing, because who'd want to remember dying? With the gasping and the leaking and the fluids and all? Even if you go quietly in your sleep, it can be a bit disgusting. And if you died violently, no way do you want to hold on to the fear and confusion and pain.

How I died is almost a total blank. Almost. I think there were yellow leaves. Fuzzy flakes crisscrossing a big shadow in my left eye. Something silver. All in all, not very much.

I should say that once you get completely clean, you leave here for Garden Hills. It's somewhere up beyond the slopes from where I am now. Nobody says much about Garden Hills because you don't come back from it. All I really know is that you come to Port Haven, you forget forget forget, then you go up there.

For . . . *ever!*

•   •   •

GeeGee walks to the shore each day to welcome the dinghies and kayaks, battleships and cruise liners that dock here with each new batch of souls. It's how I first met her. When I paddled ashore (it was a slow death day) I was seven and didn't know anybody. I never knew her when I was alive, but GeeGee welcomed me and was nice and became my closest friend here.

That's one of the great things about Port Haven. You get to know people you didn't when you were alive, and they're all pretty nice to you. Strolling the streets with GeeGee like I am now makes me feel warm inside. She gives off a scent like a just-peeled orange. It's a happy smell. And she has a glow, soft and almost musical, that she wraps me up in. GeeGee makes me feel safe.

Myself, I don't normally watch for boats. I'm not expecting anyone. But I'm heading to the shore today because, over the last week, I've been attacked by noises clawing the inside of my head. After five years with GeeGee I was just getting to where I was clearing out and calming down. I was on track. The yellow leaves and the thing in my eye were getting so I almost didn't think about them anymore.

Then this horrible scratching begins, like tree branches tearing at your window in a storm. Like fingernails scraping through a layer of paint and showing you what lies beneath.

"It means someone has unfinished business with you,"

GeeGee said as she sat with me on my porch swing this morning. "Your mother, maybe. Or your father. Or the postman, your priest, a teacher, or the president."

I rubbed my eyebrow and smirked when she told me that. "I thought *we're* supposed to be about that. Haunting *them* and all."

GeeGee giggled then. "Ironic, isn't it?"

2

WHAT RUSSELL SAYS

I should say that Port Haven is laid out sort of like a small town, with low houses and trim lawns and shade trees. Everything's crisp and neat. There's lots of sun, the air is fresh and warm, and it's always summer but not hot summer. Early June. I like that, because it's kind of the opposite of how Pennsylvania was the November I died. November 20, two days before Thanksgiving. I only know the exact date because Russell wrote it down and told GeeGee, and she told me and I remember it.

It's complicated, but Russell once said that the instant you die, living people start to forget about you—they can't really help it—which actually jump-starts you forgetting about yourself. You keep forgetting and forgetting until your whole self fades peacefully, "like mist in the sun."

Unless, of course, you try *not* to leave, or you remember too much, or you visit the living too often. Then, Russell says, you get ripped away from here. And it hurts. "They scream, those souls do, who remain too long. You feel them getting pulled apart. Ripped right down the center!"

Icky, right?

Russell also says that the reason I'm twelve now and not still seven, which I was when I died, is because I'm a twin. As Matt ages, he keeps imagining me doing stuff with him, so even though I'm dead up here, I get older along with him—in his mind—down there. That's probably also why I'm not fading as quickly as most people. Russell says that some souls manage to stay here years and years, either because they're too famous to be forgotten or because they're waiting for someone to arrive and refusing to leave until that happens.

Maybe the most important thing Russell says is that there are bonds between all of us, the living and the not. There are, he says, "a thousand, thousand threads," binding us all in different ways, but we hardly ever realize it. "Sometimes two colors come together unexpectedly, crossing and tangling and weaving at a point no one suspects. Patterns are woven," he says, "patterns are woven and repeated, subtly or accidentally, over time and space, over many years and many places." That's all very nice, but once a thread begins to fray, the big weave loosens, and the countless threads between the living and the dead begin to pull apart.

Bottom line: after we die, you people don't remember us so much, then we forget, then we fly away to the far north, where we stay ever after. The way we're supposed to.

3

IT'S ALL ONE BIG WAR

GeeGee and I arrive at the water. A handful of people—most old, a few young—are playing volleyball on the beach.

"There's Elly or whoever," I say. "As usual."

Every time I come down here there's a girl with a crooked ponytail, building a sandcastle by herself. No one's real sure of her name, but she's almost eight, Russell told me, and I always see her playing by the water, facing the sea. No one's ever with her, and I've never actually spoken to her, but Gee-Gee tells me she's down here every day. Right now, Elly or Ellen or Ella stands.

"Looks like a warship coming in," GeeGee says.

It's an aircraft carrier the size of a floating city, and it's packed with soldiers in all different kinds of uniforms, some bearded in robes and scarves. There are mostly men, although there are more women than I would have thought. Boys and girls too.

"Must be another war somewhere," I say.

"Oh, Danny, it's all one big war."

GeeGee glances back to the veranda of the beach house. Russell's there, talking to a guy in a baseball cap who he told me once is always asking questions about his two sons.

Russell likes family stories, and, if you think about it, what *isn't* a family story? At the moment he's got his feet propped on the railing, lounging in a slanted wooden chair, his usual position while listening and scribbling notes for the book he's writing.

As you can probably guess, he calls it *A Thousand, Thousand Threads.*

GeeGee reaches up to smooth my left eyebrow, but she can't hide the nick in it. "Shall we ask Russell about your noises before you go off and hurt yourself? He knows oh so much."

It's not well known, but we have two ways to visit the before place. Variety is the spice of death, they say. One method gives us pretty bad headaches. The other does something much worse. I go for the headache today.

"You know, GeeGee, I gotta see what it is myself. I'll do the grotto, find out what I can, then ask Russell if I have questions."

"You can go on your own, then? I remember the grotto being somewhat unpleasant."

"I'm good, GeeGee. See you in a bit."

Just east of the harbor lies a craggy place with a natural arch, where water flows deep under the rocks. I don't know what its real name is, but we call it the grotto. There's a sort of swirling mist in there, eerie and mysterious, but if you stare into it hard enough, you can see the other side, your side. I climb down the rocks, focus, and try to burn through the fog, like I have X-ray vision. *Zzzz!* My head instantly starts throbbing, but after a minute, the mist begins to thin.

I see a room. A school classroom.

There's a broad oak desk with a man in a sport jacket standing behind it. He's pressing his hands flat on the desktop. His face is red. His hair is disheveled. His glasses are slipping down to the tip of his nose.

Teetering in front of the desk is a student with long hair. I ease around to the side to see the kid. My heart does a little skippy thing.

The boy's features are identical to mine. His mouth is hanging open. He's trembling, like he's going to explode.

He's my brother, Matt.

4

MAD MATT

Because visiting the before place slows down the process of "getting clean," I haven't really looked in on my brother. It's not forbidden—hey, we have free will here—but, as Russell points out, it's not encouraged. So when I see Matt after five years, I'm stunned. He has long hair, his face is narrow and pale, and he's got pimples, which, lucky me, I never did.

Matt is mumbling at his teacher—"I . . . I needed to . . . There was . . . See"—but mostly he's just shaking, not making sense. Plus, he's waving around a roll of papers like a light-saber.

Yes, I remember Star Wars. This is death, not 1950.

There are sparks shooting out of Matt's face, his head and shoulders. No one can see them but me, these bolts of energy. They're what people are feeling, their emotions. Everybody has sparks, but only souls can see them, and right now, Matt is an exploding weapons dump. His teacher just takes it, waiting for the end of Matt's nonsensical word salad.

Of course, I can hear what my brother is *actually* trying to say. His words are jumbled, but because I'm dead and his twin, I understand, just like I can see the energy he's spraying off.

What he's saying is exactly what he's been grinding into my head for the last week, and I finally hear it in words.

"Denis! My dead brother! Denis!"

I'm like, Seriously? You just realized I'm gone?

Anyway, the sight of this standoff is freaking the class out. They're in various stages of shock or disgust. All except one kid, who's not shocked but concerned, really worried.

This kid is a boy. Or maybe a girl. Honestly, this person could be either. The face has smooth cheeks, a thin nose, large brown eyes, pink lips, short hair. I read off a paper on the desk that its owner's name is Trey, but since I really can't tell whether Trey is a boy or a girl, I won't say *he* or *she*, I'll just call Trey *Trey*, and see how that works.

So while Matt continues his garbled croaking, and the teacher continues to keep his cool, Trey gets up from Trey's seat. Or almost gets up. Just sort of hovers, halfway standing, leaning, almost reaching for Matt, until the girl in the desk behind yanks Trey by the belt loop.

"Don't," the girl whispers. "You'll get in trouble like last time."

I find I can read *Trey*, too. This is one of the absolute niftiest features of being a spirit because it really helps fill in the context. It turns out "last time" was a stormy day last week—right when the scritching and scratching in my head started, by the way—when Matt angrily threw a pencil, and it turned out to be in the general direction of a teacher. *That* teacher didn't coolly wait for Matt to exhaust himself. *That* teacher got angry, and when Trey scooted up to be with Matt, the teacher took the move as joining the rebellion, and they both got detentions. Our parents and Trey's dad had to come to school.

But this time, no.

Trey allows the girl in the seat behind to tug on the belt loop until Trey sits back down.

Finally, this teacher is pretty awesome about the whole business. "I'm sorry," he calmly says three times, "but, Matt, you shouldn't have been in the teachers' lounge. And certainly not to use the copier. For now, please sit. We'll discuss it later."

The other students give the teacher a quick round of applause. I clap too, but there's no sound when I do it. Finally, the bell rings and the kids empty out. Matt lingers to talk to the teacher, but the teacher just waves him out.

"Don't do it again," he says. "And calm yourself down. Please."

"Thanks," Matt replies, his first intelligible word.

In the hall Matt and Trey immediately start whispering in each other's ears. They're zingy. On the scale of sparks, *zingies* are a strange kind of intense blue, which means you're deep, deep friends. The two of them rub shoulders in the hall and bump each other when they don't have to. Most kids don't give them a second look, while others stare at them, like they're not sure about it. Matt and Trey don't seem to care either way.

It's right about then that I feel my eyes go out of focus—visiting gives you such a brain pain, you can't do it for long—and I'm back at the grotto, the morning sun in my face.

GeeGee is standing next to me. She smiles and places her hand on my forehead, which she likes to do now and then to check on me. "I'm sorry I fell asleep. Do you feel better?"

"Me? I'm okay. It's my brother. For some reason Matt is all about me after five years."

"If he thinks about you so much, you should go to him for real."

"I don't know, GeeGee, the grotto is bad, but the way people talk about the razor scares me."

The razor, you should know, is our *other* way to visit your world.

"Besides, it's dangerous, isn't it?"

She wrinkles her nose. "He'll keep bugging you until you have to go. I did it once or twice, it's nasty, but you're young and you'll survive. The razor's the only way to actually talk to him."

Sure enough, like with most things GeeGee tells me, she's right. Before the day is over, Matt's scraping has turned to moaning, and the moaning to screaming, and the screaming to shrieking.

"Denis! Denis! *Denisssss!*"

I have to respond.

If I want to stay sane.

Which I kind of do.

5

HOME FIRES

That night the beach in Port Haven is calm.

I'm not.

Matt's gotten noisier by the minute. I'm still terrified of the razor, so even though my brain pounds inside my skull, like it's trying to get out, I have another go at the grotto to see if I can discover what my brother's suddenly so cranky about.

I find Matt with Mom and Dad in our living room in Buckwood, which is in Pennsylvania. The TV is off. The three of them are staring zombielike at the blank screen. I don't know how long they've been doing this, but if the classroom was tense, this is a war zone. In the silence I scan the room. No photographs of family, as you might see in other homes, and I remember it was always that way. This explains something, but I'm not sure what.

All at once Mom bolts to her feet, like a corpse bursting from her grave, but then slumps back to the couch like a dropped sandbag. Her body is shooting black sparks in every direction. It bites me somewhere deep in the chest to see her like this, and I understand why we're not encouraged to visit.

Mom has gotten far older than five years should have made her. The smile she used to give me and Matt is stone gone. It's not in her face anymore. She's thin—as if she eats only enough to keep her moving. Her cheeks have caved in; her hair is streaked with gray. She's what, forty, forty-one? I try to imagine her arms around me now, and there isn't any warmth there. There is only grief. Her eyes are dead when she turns them to Dad.

He presses his fingers against his temples and flicks a look at Matt, who is buried in a soft chair. Dad is a broad-shouldered man who works outside, real physical, but the afternoon joker I remember is as gone as Mom's smile. If Dad is grieving, it's a different kind than hers. He is smoldering inside, quivering. His sparks are angry and hot, darts of dark light firing off him like sniper bullets. He carries a heavy weight on his shoulders, which I have to think is me.

Seeing them like this, in my old home, I'm slapped in the face to remember how our family—Matt, me, my mom, and my dad—were in line to be really happy.

It wasn't like one twin got all the smarts or looks. We both got plenty. Matt was musical. I ran fast. Matt was the better reader and test taker. I was way funnier and inventive and had clever ideas. I gather Dad wasn't superhappy when he was young, though I never knew why, but his job as manager of a landscaping company was solid, and he liked being outside in the weather. He was good at it, too. Mom worked part-time in our school library, did story times and read-alouds with the younger kids. She could be anything, really, but she wanted to be near us. We ate together every night. We took vacations. We had fun.

It was a small life, I guess, but it was sweet and moving forward, until the day I got sick or had an accident or drowned or whatever I did, and all the good stuff was kicked off the edge of a cliff.

As I hover over the scene now, I notice what I didn't in class—Matt's hair is not only long, it's greasy, like he rubs grease in it. Clusters of pimples dot his cheeks, and his fingernails are bitten down to the quick. I honestly can't figure why Trey hangs out with him.

"Matt, explain it to me again?" Mom says, breaking the silence. "When your teacher called, he was really sympathetic, but I didn't understand what he was saying you did? I know he could have sent you to the office, but he didn't. What exactly did you do?"

Matt turns to Dad, who might understand but just sits

there staring at the floor. Matt doesn't answer.

"Why did you go into the teachers' lounge, of all places?" Mom goes on. "You can't . . . What's happened with you over the last couple of weeks, Matt? Your schoolwork is suffering. . . ."

In his mind Matt is reading the papers he made copies of in the lounge, the papers he shook at his teacher and that are now hidden in a box under his bed. They seem official and have marks stamped on them and seals—like school forms or doctor reports.

"I was . . . upset," Matt says weakly.

"Obviously," Mom snaps. "Mr. Brown said you were shaking. Are you coming down with something?" She leans forward, wanting to reach out and touch his forehead like GeeGee touches mine, but not doing it. "Maybe you picked up something at St. Francis last week."

I sense from Matt's sudden thoughts about a trumpet that St. Francis is a hospice in Buckwood and that the school band gave a performance there.

Dad lifts his head. "It isn't that, Bonnie. He's . . . Matt, you've been looking at maps, haven't you?"

Mom falls back into the couch, as if out of breath. "Maps? Of what? Oh. No, Matt. You can just forget anything to do with that. Maps!"

She purses her lips tightly, suddenly goes cold, like a switch has just been flipped. "Well, I'm glad you didn't get another detention. That's all I have to say. You can go to your room now, Matt. Bed. No phone." She nods toward the stairs and folds her arms over her chest with a quiver. Matt excuses himself, walks upstairs to his room.

Maps? Really? I thought maps were a good thing. They tell you where things are and stuff.

I search my parents, from one to the other. It's hard to look them in the face. My dad is barely recognizable. I don't know if he's lifted his head once since I got here. And Mom. She's a block of ice. Angry ice, if ice can be angry, and so cold inside.

Without a word, she flicks off the lamp nearest her, sits for a moment, waiting for something from my dad that doesn't come, then leaves the room and drags herself up the stairs step by step, like she's carrying a body and can't put it down.

"I'm sorry, Mom," I whisper as she passes. "I love you."

Of course she doesn't hear me.

Lights go off, one then another, around the house.

After sitting silently for a half hour, fingering the television remote but not using it, Dad trudges up the steps. Strange how going upstairs at the end of the day is so hard for them.

He changes out of his clothes and lies down in bed next to my mom, careful not to disturb her, though she's not sleeping and probably can't, because her mind is a swirl of dark, churning water.

6

THE UNFINISHED WORK

I shift my gaze to Matt's room. So easy to do. He lies awake, listening to the dying sounds of the house. The creak of floorboards, the hum of the hot water pipes. It's dark in his room except for a mini flashlight lying in the folds of his blanket. Hearing nothing but the settling house, he quietly slides a flat box out from under his bed.

It's then that I see *my* bed, the bed I slept in until I died. It's still pushed against the inside wall, made neatly and unslept in. It's been empty for five years, but it's still there.

Matt doesn't give it a glance as he mouths the flashlight and burrows out of the box several folded maps, a couple of old books, and the papers from school today.

Unfolding a map, he studies it under the light. He can't

see me, of course. I'm still watching from the misty grotto. Matt won't see me unless I haunt him for real, which I don't know I'll try, despite what GeeGee says. I'm only observing him trace his fingers across a map covered in lines and curved arrows. It's a Civil War battlefield. Pennsylvania has a couple. This is Gettysburg, the most famous. I've never gone there, though he might have, since.

So what's the deal? Is he studying for a history test in the dark? Why is this a secret? Mom freaked out when Dad said he was looking at maps. What's wrong with maps?

Then he flips open a book to a photograph of one of the monuments on the battlefield, a big block of dark stone, and it's like someone smacks me across the face.

The tall dark shape standing against the sky reminds me of that vertical form I see floating at the edge of my vision, the line or shape that's lingered out of focus at the corner of my left eye since I got to Port Haven. I don't know if it has to do with the scar across my eyebrow, but sometimes grainy flecks move across the lens. If I ever thought it was just some weird eye problem, seeing this monument now, I'm not so sure.

From the dark, the darker darkness rises.

As he tugs out the sheaf of papers from this morning, he taps his cell phone—disobeying what our mom commanded—and Trey, his short-haired friend from class, picks up.

"So I put the originals back," Matt whispers. "I don't think Dad will know I made copies. And I was right. There's something here no one *ever* told me. *Ever.*" He pauses. "Trey?"

"I'm fine, how are you?" There's the sound of a smirk in Trey's voice. I like Trey already, and I sense that Trey has been there for Matt in ways I've never been.

"Sorry, it's . . ." Matt stops and listens. "Hold on."

He sets down the phone, drags the rug to the door, rolls the end over, and gently tucks it against the bottom to block any light or sound. He takes up the phone again.

"Two things. Of all the dozens of state monuments at Gettysburg, the police found Denis at the Georgia one. I was never told that. They just said Gettysburg and changed the subject."

Wait, what? *Police*? Police *found me*? What was I doing, just wandering around?

"They were shielding you from it," Trey says softly. "How do you tell a seven-year-old they found his brother that way on some old battlefield?"

Time-out! Found his brother *"that way"*? What way? What are you two talking about?

"Yeah, but out of all the states, Georgia!" Matt goes on, as if that's the important part of what he's just said. "Dad was *born* in Georgia. He's *from* there! It's got to be a huge clue."

Except, hello—*I never went to Gettysburg!*

"And here's another thing I never knew," Matt adds.

"According to one report, there was a maroon compact car parked on a road about a mile away. Which means the killer carried the bod—carried Denis—all the way across a field to put him at the monument..."

Killer? Body?

I'm getting sick to the stomach I don't have.

"If you have a map, it's halfway down the Confederate line, between Pitzer Woods and Warfield Ridge," Matt adds. "Whoever it was had to hike a long way. But why all the trouble? There's a parking lot right across the road."

"Didn't the cops investigate the Georgia thing?"

"Yeah, but hardly deep enough. It says, quote, the victim's father has not returned to Georgia for a period of several years. The victim's mother has no ties to the state. Other alibis check out. Unquote. That's it. But, like, I don't know *anything* about when my dad lived there. Plus, he was stationed in Georgia in the army. It could be one of his war buddies, getting back at us."

My dad was in the army?

"Your dad was in the army?"

"You don't listen, Trey. I told you this. He was in for two years, doing his training at Fort Benning, which is in Georgia. That was a couple of years before he married my mom."

"Good lead," Trey says. "We definitely have to find out more. So did you get in trouble for making the copies?"

"Eh, not too much. I'm still on Mom's sort-of good side

for my gig at the hospice with the band. I don't think my dad cares about it so much. Or something. It's like he's not here."

I can't read the fine print, but arrayed on Matt's bed next to the police reports are several yellowed newspapers.

BUCKWOOD BOY MISSING SINCE SUNDAY

THIRD GRADER FOUND DEAD AFTER THREE DAYS

BODY OF SEVEN-YEAR-OLD DISCOVERED AT
GETTYSBURG PARK

COMMUNITY MOURNS LOST TWIN OF PERRY
STUDENT

I shudder to imagine the stories. The police effort, the quickly organized volunteers, the widening scope of the investigation, the innumerable posters of my face tacked up on poles and inside shop windows, the horrifying hours Matt and my parents spent waiting, the bizarre finding of my body, the crushing darkness that fell afterward, all because of me. My memory burns. This is all about me, but I don't remember any of it. I wasn't there for it. I've been utterly blindsided.

"Text me a pic of the monument"—Trey yawns—"and my superior mind will study it for clues."

"Show you in the morning. Somebody's coming down the hall. Probably Mom to check on me. Bye."

Matt ends the call. I look down over his shoulder at a

photograph from the police file. I see my little face, my lifeless body huddled against the base of the Georgia monument. I feel pummeled in the head. I was lost. I was missing. Then my *body* was *found* at Gettysburg battlefield three days later? That's clear across the state from Buckwood!

Matt quickly stuffs the papers, maps, and books in the box and pushes it under his bed. He switches off the flashlight, tugs the rug back with his heel, and goes still. Mom quietly opens his door, peeks in, closes it.

I rub my eyebrow as I hear Matt ticking one thought over in his mind.

Georgia. Georgia. Georgia.

7

REMEMBER ME

I storm away from the grotto and wander the streets of Port Haven, up and down, rolling the whole gruesome mess over in my mind. I'm shocked, stunned, sick in my gut.

Murdered.

I was murdered.

Naturally, GeeGee won't remember my death. She knows I'm close to my anniversary, but she's lost most recent history and is getting spottier all the time. But what about the things I remember? *Is* there something silver about how I died? Where are the yellow leaves, and the dark thing in the corner of my vision? Where was I floating and drowning? A pool? A beach?

Do all of these visions combine—weave together—to point to my murder?

When I ask Russell, he says he *might* have written *something* down when I first arrived and there *may* be a clue there, but maybe *not*, if it wasn't *appropriate* for the book he's trying to write, and anyway he writes *very* small and scratchily and his eyesight is *rather* failing so it would take *so* long to find it that it's *hardly* worth looking. I'm paraphrasing here.

Over the next few days, I become addicted to the grotto, headaching myself inside out as I listen to Matt explain each new thing to Trey.

How finding the police file flooded everything back to Matt in sobbing, breathless memories. The inhuman crush of reporters at the house. The dumb shock of the neighbor kids, as if *their* brother was missing, or that it was somehow Matt's fault, which he almost came to believe. The thousand kind and hopeful and meaningless words from hundreds of people he didn't know.

How three full days passed between when I went missing from an amusement park called Funland near a town called Hunker on Sunday, and when some tourist from Atlanta screamed bloody murder at Gettysburg the following Wednesday, the day before Thanksgiving.

How for all the time I was missing, every hour for three days and nights, the light on my porch in Buckwood stayed lit, as if to light me the way home, and how it was turned off when my parents got the call from the police and drove to identify my little body.

How the weather on the day the police found me, and the previous days, had been clear and dry in Gettysburg, but my clothes were wet, with a sour, musty smell, which suggested to the police that I wasn't killed near the battlefield.

How the coroner decided the condition of my body put my actual death on Tuesday—the day *before* I was found and two days *after* I went missing. How besides my broken neck, they'd found "nonlethal bruising" on my shoulders and head, and I had recently lost a tooth.

Over the days, I can't help studying the police file that Matt copied in the teachers' lounge, and each time I'm stricken to see my young self—seven-year-old Denis Richard Egan, sitting with my back against the monument, my face tilted up, eyes closed, my right cheek on the base's top edge. Except for the strange angle of my head, it looked like I was simply tired, had just paused to rest, and had fallen asleep.

"There's something else," Matt tells Trey one night on the phone, "that nobody but my parents and the police know about. Denis had only one shoe on."

One shoe!

"He's wearing one sneaker. His right foot is bare. His sole had been scraped, but the bruises had been cleaned, the coroner said, and one cut even had a bandage on it."

"Wow . . . ," Trey whispers. "Why didn't that get into the papers?"

"The police must have thought it could lead them to the killer. Dad was probably crazy about it, how it was another clue," Matt whispers, then adds, "The police never found his sneaker."

I stare at the photographs and cry. Yes, the dead can cry. My seven-year-old body looks so frail set against the big hulking monument. It was a frigid morning when I was found, but the sun was out, and the sky was as blue as sapphire, one newspaper said.

Matt spreads other file photos out on his bed. Police cars and emergency vans parked askew on the grass. Tall screens angled around me. Medical personnel with paper shoe covers.

"The whole investigation went cold," Matt says, "until two months ago. It was bizarre here at the time. My parents knew, but I never got the full story until now. Listen."

Matt unfolds another newspaper, from this past July, and he reads it out to Trey. The gist is that a couple of teenagers were swimming in an abandoned limestone quarry near the Youghiogheny River. One of the boys dove off a rock, hooting and laughing—I can almost hear him doing that. His name was Brendan, but his friends and parents call him Bo. Bo took a running leap at the middle of the pond and broke his ankle when he crashed into something under the surface. He was all right, on crutches for two months, but when the police investigated, they found the rusted hulk of an old maroon Honda submerged in the quarry.

Hearing about it on the news, the Buckwood cop assigned to my case, Detective Edwin Sparn, looked back into the almost-five-year-old cold case because he remembered that the car seen early that morning parked on Millerstown Road in Gettysburg was described as "a maroon compact."

Even though the quarry was nearly two hundred miles from the battlefield, Detective Sparn decided the car they pulled out of the water was very likely the same car, mostly because the Youghiogheny is only thirty or so minutes from Funland, where I was last seen alive.

The Honda was reported stolen from a parking lot in New Castle.

"When Detective Sparn called the house to say they'd identified the car," Matt tells Trey, "my dad screamed, 'They found the car! Bonnie, they found the car!' 'What car?' I asked them. But Mom goes, 'It's not the car,' without missing a beat, as if she'd been waiting every day for news and had an answer ready. 'It *is* the car,' Dad told her. 'Ed thinks so—'

"'Even if it is the car, how does it help?' Mom said. Then she got up from the kitchen table, stood there, her face all gray. 'My God, Gary,' she said. 'You were moving on. We just got to a place where we could breathe again. Where I could think about Denis as a baby, the funny things he did that were just his own. Now this, the stupid car? And he's dead all over again. Let Denis go. He's in a better place. He's not with us anymore. He's gone.'

"Dad looked at me then," Matt tells Trey. "He was stunned or something and didn't say anything, so Mom bolted from the room. She hadn't even finished eating. Not a word about the car since then."

"Whoa," Trey says. "That's hard."

I'm listening to Matt, and I get that what Mom had said to Dad was harsh, but I sort of agree with her. After years underwater, of course, there was no evidence left in the Honda—neither blood nor my sneaker nor the missing tooth—so finding the stolen car went as nowhere as everything else.

Mom was right about me being gone, too.

I'd been up here nearly five years when that conversation happened, walking the streets day after day in the sun with GeeGee, playing ball, shooting hoops with old pro-basketball players kept alive by sports fans. But now that I hear the grim facts of the police file, I wonder:

Did I know what was happening to me?

How long was I conscious before I died?

I must have been terrified out of my mind.

8

THE PURPOSE OF DEATH

When I trudge up the sand, exhausted from my latest stint at the grotto, GeeGee is sitting on the veranda of the beach club. She is not alone.

Every day, after watching the boats come in, she plays cards with Russell and a couple of the other souls. I've seen them every now and then read one of Russell's old books. Or try to.

They're some bunch, these souls.

One is a loud man with a crest of hot pink hair. The other is a lady in big black medical sunglasses who complains about everything. I call her Frannie McFrown. Together they play a game called bridge, and every time I hear them announce a fresh game, I find myself remembering bridges.

As usual Russell's up there with GeeGee, but he's not playing this time. He sits with his arms around his knees, looking out over the water.

"I'm still in shock," I say after I tell them what I discovered.

"Well, of course you are, dear boy. Murder!" Russell says, unhugging his knees and jotting this down in his notebook. "Do be careful, though. The more you get drawn into their life down there, the worse it is for you up here. The purpose of death, as you know, is to become clean. As clean as clear glass. I'm sure there is a technical term I've forgotten, but that's what Port Haven is all about. The mess down below will taint you. As fascinating as they can be, all those threads ensnare you. You get soiled, and you drag that up here. No, no. There's a proper time for each of us to fade and pass away. I've told you the danger of staying down there too long."

"Pish-posh," GeeGee says with a kind of pleasant scowl. "You should visit your brother for real now. There's only so much you can do by watching through a fog. I would go again right now, but no one wants an old dead woman lurking behind the curtains. You . . . you could do some good."

"I say stay away," says Pink Hair, strolling over from the card table with a pitying look. "You get *full* down there, like you just swallowed five potatoes. Once you do, the razor'll cut you up nasty, and you'll rip in half when your time comes." He sets his face in a know-it-all expression.

"Rip in half?" I ask.

"Rip, rip, rip!" he says, as if he couldn't wait for me to ask. "And you should hear the screaming. Huh-uh, Buster, it ain't going to do you no good messing around down there."

And the word *ain't* suddenly shoots through me like a jolt of electricity.

I hear it deep in my ears, a cruel voice: angry, nasty, distant, long ago.

Ain't.

I wonder. Near the end, in my last days alive, did someone say the word *ain't* to me?

"Russell?"

"Mmm?"

"What does it mean if instead of forgetting, you start to remember things?"

"Ho-ho! It means you're getting dirty again," Pink Hair butts in. "You're getting confused and heavy. It means you're bucking the system, Frankie. You don't want to be a mingler."

"Mingler?"

Pink Hair sneers. "A crosser. A laggard."

"Those are unpleasant words," GeeGee says. "Even for you, sonny boy."

Pink Hair shrugs. "A mingler stays too long, gets filthy. Up here, you forget and get clean. They planned it so you forget. That's the point. To be all innocent to get back in. Why you think they call it *Garden* Hills? Plus, they need homes for all the other souls coming here. Look—another cruise liner. See what I mean?"

GeeGee wrinkles her wrinkled face at Pink Hair. "They're not *homes* we live in, dear boy, they're *houses*. And that isn't the reason anyway. It's simply the right thing for us older folks to become one with the universe. But, David, you were so young, poor dear. I've tried to tell you things, and teach you what I know before I forget."

"You do teach me, GeeGee. You tell me lots. Birds and the names of things. Plants. Words and what they mean. Things about weather and people. Grown-up stuff."

"But I never really knew Matt," she says. "Not as I know you. That's always made me a little sad. Don't you feel that, too?" She eyes the nick in my eyebrow and reaches a finger toward it, then lowers it. "Your brother won't stop haunting you until you go down for real. He must need you desperately. That's reason enough to go."

"*He's* haunting *you*. A plot twist!" Russell writes that, too.

"Well, he's sure making my death miserable," I say. "With all the noise, I can barely hear you guys anymore. I guess I have to go."

"It won't do you no good," Pink Hair repeats. "Believe me, it's an unkind world for some of us."

"It's true the razor will hurt," GeeGee says, and places her palm against my forehead. "But doing it once is all right. And what a dear boy you are to want to visit your twin brother."

9

COUNTERATTACK

Once I decide to take the plunge, they're all excited to pitch in with advice, especially GeeGee.

"You have to plan these things," she says, "and you have to do it in stages, or the shock can kill the poor dears, simply kill them dead. It has happened."

"Or he could combust," Pink Hair says, and I wonder how he cannot know that people think he talks too much. He plops down at the nearby card table and shuffles two decks into one. "Boom! Game over. If your daddy isn't ready, that is."

"My brother," I say. "And he's so ready."

"All right, then," GeeGee says. "Let's start with three visitations. I've always liked going from public to private."

"I agree," Russell says, repositioning himself at the card table now and cutting the cards, which he passes back to Pink Hair, who shuffles them again.

It seems to me that in all the times I've come here, I've never actually seen them play bridge. They just shuffle and deal, then shuffle and deal again. I think they've forgotten the rules.

"The first time you show yourself, make it startling," Russell advises, "but a bit vague. This tells him to be on guard, but if nothing else happens, he simply forgets."

"Get his attention for a moment, then stand aside," Gee-Gee adds. "Be gentle about it. If your brother's as sensitive a boy as you are, Donald, he'll be stupefied!"

Russell nods. "Exactly. For number two, I'd suggest an incident a bit more intense, but still brief. Just enough to give him a pitter-patter in his bowels. Finally, a private place—"

"Not a bathroom," laughs Pink Hair. "That's a hotbed of problems, let me tell you!"

"Perhaps his room at home is best?" GeeGee offers.

"Just so," says Russell. "This is where you finally reveal who you are. Allow him to be surprised, but not in front of anyone, so you control the scene. You simply confront him and say, 'Hello, Marcus!'"

"Matt. I'm going to visit Matt."

"And if *Matt* doesn't want to believe it," Russell says, "you remind him of the first two times. 'Do you recall when

I tripped you in chapel, or the time I pulled your braid on the polo field?' That sort of thing. You need to prime the pump. By the third time, you've got him. You tell him in no uncertain terms, 'Stop haunting me!' That'll set him straight. Then you come back, forget all about it, and get pure."

"Sounds good to me," I say. "Murder is icky, and this noise in my head is scrambling my brain."

GeeGee is nodding through this, and finally, so are Pink Hair and Frannie McFrown, who has just joined the table and is building a house from the cards that Pink Hair has just dealt.

"So," GeeGee says, "what is Matt's life like? Where does he go, what does he do? Give us the details, as they say."

I think about it. "Well, there's our house, his friend Trey's house—you'd like Trey, GeeGee—also the woods and streets between the two houses, the neighborhood—Matt bikes lots of places—the school, sports stuff. He plays trumpet in the school band. Plus, he must go to the library to look up old newspapers. My death was reported in lots of them."

GeeGee beams. "First stop, band practice. So much wind is blowing around that room, you'll be right at home."

"But keep it simple. Don't appear to anyone but him, and don't stay long," Russell warns, tapping his finger on his notebook. "Glide through, try not to use your senses. The more you see and feel, the heavier you become, and, well, I wouldn't risk it. You can't do the razor more than a few times. I did once or twice. This young lady here has too, if I recall."

"I have," GeeGee says, almost shyly. "You don't want to anymore, though. Not at my age."

"And watch out for encampments," Pink Hair adds. "Rippety-rip-rip!"

"Encampments? What do you mean?"

Pink Hair just chuckles to himself, while Russell's face manages to pale even more. "What our friend is referring to are those grim places where souls are trapped, unable to wrench themselves free to return. Finally, however, the process overtakes them. Violently. And minglers are forced to return here. Stay clear of such places, for your own health."

"Remain a few hours at most," GeeGee adds. "You must protect yourself."

"Thanks, GeeGee," I say. "I love you. Please don't go anywhere while I'm down there."

She pats my cheek, checks my forehead again. "Oh, it isn't up to me, dear. Put in a good word for me down there, though, will you? Slow things down a bit. So I can spend more time with you . . . Oh, I do love you . . . mmm . . . which one are you again?"

I put my arms around her shoulders and they seem so slight, they almost fold under me, like paper.

"Denis," I whisper in her ear. "I'm Denis."

And my heart, or whatever is in there, aches.

10

THE RAZOR

Next morning I wake early, Matt's voice having dragged nails across my brain all night. Following a winding path into the foothills that GeeGee and Russell told me about, I hike up to the very edge of Port Haven. It gets colder with every step, and I know Garden Hills is just beyond the crest, but luckily, I find what I'm looking for at the end of a narrow trail—a large dented metal structure like an abandoned utility shed.

This is where they keep the razor.

I know the stories—Russell and GeeGee have both told me what they know, Pink Hair, too, of course—but I find out soon enough that grotto-gazing is cheesecake compared to this.

After nudging through the iron door into the dark—it's not locked; that would be cruel—you close it behind you, draw in a breath, and pretty much die again.

They call it the razor because when you pass into the other life, it's like pushing yourself face-first into a tall vertical razor that stretches from your head to the floor. Imagine slicing yourself in half and reassembling on the other side of the blade, which, by the way, burns like a hot wire.

This is just what the razor feels like, you understand. There's no real seven-foot-tall blade anywhere in heaven, because that would be not only uncool, but insane. We're souls, not bodies. But this is what it feels like.

So I do it.

I slice myself in half.

Since it's my first time, it takes longer and hurts more than I feared. I'm sure they design it that way to keep people from haunting somebody for a joke. We don't have bodies, but with the razor, you're convinced you have one, and you feel every fiber of it as one by one your nerves are severed. You feel as if you leave bits of yourself on the blade, tissue and sinew, except you don't want to look back to see.

But I do it for Matt. I do it for Matt, I tell myself, because I'm such a good brother. I want to see him and spend an hour or two with him, before I tell him off and jet back to Port Haven to come clean. But I do it for myself, too. If I really *was* murdered—which I still can't believe—don't I need to know more, even if it hurts?

Can I leave the awful thing alone? Can I really move on before discovering what these things mean?

Yellow leaves.

The shadow in my eye.

Floating and drowning.

Ain't.

I feel altered after the razor—sad, sick, even ashamed. It takes some minutes before I can focus my eyes and see where I am.

A narrow rain-wet street of squat two-story houses with attics. Some have front porches, rough driveways, and detached single-car garages. Most have peeling paint or buckled siding, overgrown lawns, untrimmed shrubs, all of it so different from the neatness of Port Haven.

The road is paved, but potholed and uneven. Litter collects in the gutters. It's a gray little street like millions of others, I guess, but I remember it. More than that, I *feel* this street. I see it and smell it. I hear it and touch it and taste it in my mouth. I know I shouldn't, but I do.

It's where I used to live.

||

BUCKWOOD

Buckwood's not all the way awake.

It's late September, barely summer anymore, but the air hasn't turned yet. That will change. A cool wind will steal in one night, and October will be here. Then November will fall over the town like iron, hard and cold. Ugly November. I hate November.

I know I'm supposed to forget all of this, but it rushes at me like a herd of horses, and I'm suddenly afraid to forget. What's happening to GeeGee is sad, and it scares me. I don't want to drift off into the hills. I know in my soul that remembering is against the rules, and what Russell said haunts me like a mantra. *The purpose of death is to become clean. There's a proper time for each of us to fade and pass away.* But being here again, I crave for people to think of me, love me, keep me dead in their hearts and minds. I didn't get enough of that when I was alive because I wasn't around long enough.

That's what hurts me now.

Get clean of everything, forget the funkiness of life, flee from the clutter in the world you lived in—that's what Pink Hair and the others were on about. Shower off the sloppy jumble of life, the smell, the taste, and touch of it, sure, that's the law. But I'm standing on the bit of crooked sidewalk running the length of my front yard, and I can see each weed and blade of crabgrass sprouting in the cracks. A crumpled coffee cup lies in the gutter, a plastic wrapper, the stalk of a pen. The band of lawn between the walk and the street needs serious trimming. So does the yard. The grass is ragged. I practically hear it growing. I know Dad is a landscaper, and this can't be good for business, but it's like nobody cares enough because they can't care enough because they're too busy dealing with the junk of having to be alive.

I don't know. I don't, but right now, I feel sad to have left it all.

My room, the room I shared with Matt, is in the corner on the left on the second floor. One window looks south, the other west. The front one gets the morning light at an angle.

The house faces pinewoods and a range of blue hills. Because the rising sun is behind them, the hills are even bluer this morning. The gables of our house are just beginning to catch the orange light. They'll turn yellow, then white when the full sun rises.

This is the happy house I grew up in, and now its rafters are shaking with pain.

A gray pickup slows carefully at the stop sign. The willow in the side yard Matt and I used to climb barely holds its leaves. We'd play detective in the woods beyond, find each other, hide again, making a game in what we thought were big woods but that now look sparse.

There's a familiar click, and our front door opens. Mom whooshes down the steps, dressed for work. Her face is blank. The pickup drives away from the stop sign. In a few quick moves, Mom is in her car, starts, backs out onto the street, and drives off as if she's left an empty house.

In fact, both Matt and my father are inside.

Maybe Dad is still hunched over breakfast.

Matt could be pulling his school junk together. In a few minutes he'll say some words to Dad, leave the house, hop on his bike. He lives too close to school to rate a stop on the bus route. Mom doesn't work at the school library anymore, but an hour away in Pittsburgh. It's a matter of minutes one way or the other if she breezes into work or gets stuck in traffic. I sense all of this.

Matt probably doesn't mind the twelve minutes of solitary biking to school. It's a dark, sticky web of tension in the house. Hard to take and easy to leave.

I don't want to go in.

I walk.

If you take a left at our mailbox, go to the end of the street, and take another left for three blocks, you'll find yourself on Woodrell Avenue. It runs through the middle of Buckwood. Take it east for five blocks and go left before the brick offices and shops begin. Vlautin Road comes up about a half mile on your right. Down a little more and you reach Buckwood Middle School, where I would have gone with Matt.

I could be there in a split second, but I take my time, draw in the town as it slowly blinks its eyes open and stirs. I shouldn't, but on sidewalk after broken sidewalk I let the sights and sounds and smells of a small town overwhelm me.

Some thirty slow minutes later, I arrive at the school. A couple of cars are pulling into the very far spaces of the lot. Soon after, a pair of old-guy custodians, some young men with tattooed arms in kitchen whites, a young woman carrying a stepladder, and three mom-age women collect in the circle, before slipping in through a single open door.

More cars enter. A couple of teachers in sweaters stroll down the sidewalk from a nearby neighborhood. A dark blue sedan pulls into a spot near the front of the lot, and out jumps a zippy woman in a gray jacket who, showering easy sparks on everyone and saying nine things at the same time, I take to be the principal.

I round the parking lot three times. I'm sucking up the vibes, tensions, the often funny ways a school opens for the day. It's all movement and life. I know I shouldn't be, but I'm sad again, this time that I never got to go here.

Young women get out of small new cars, second-career men in family cars—these are more teachers and aides. I know these things about them because they're light inside.

Gradually, the lot clutters and fills. One of those custodians reappears with a kitchen lady. He unlocks the other five front doors as she hoists the flag up the pole in the circle. The pole reminds me of that nagging vertical line on the edge of my left eye's vision, but it's not quite right.

The man, head tilted up at the rising Stars and Stripes, lights a cigarette, and something about the little white stick smoking between his fingers nags at me, but that also goes nowhere like the lost sneaker and the car in the quarry and Bo's shattered ankle.

As the sun rises on the snapping flag, I hear Matt getting near—"Denis! Georgia! *Murdered!*"—and I know I have to make it all stop or never sleep the peaceful sleep of the dead. I take a last look around, but it's time. It's time.

Wandering two floors and the many halls, longer and wider than the elementary's halls, I get lost. It happens. Plus,

I never came for orientation. I try not to feel frustrated.

By the time I locate the band room, several bells have rung. Hundreds of students have thundered down every hall. I wait for it all to dry up, wait for another bell, then whisk myself into the noisy room.

Matt is already in the second row, rolling his fingers over the buttons of his trumpet, eyeing the music on his stand.

Scanning him from every angle, I hover above the mostly empty row behind him for the longest time, running over GeeGee's and Russell's advice about how to start haunting. I decide to sit directly behind Matt and wait for the perfect opportunity to buzz him.

When I finally sit down, however, my seat is occupied.

12

A TWIN AND HIS SOLO

I'm sitting in a lap.

A girl's lap. The lap of a girl.

Brown hair. Green eyes. Long, loose braid over her left shoulder.

I know, right?

I'm seven years old and sitting on a girl, so extreme ick. But I'm also twelve or whatever, so . . . interesting. Except it suddenly gets weird—weirder—when the sax part comes along because the muscles in the girl's arms and legs tense and she raises the mouthpiece to her lips. I jump off.

Most people don't feel spirits near them, but this girl—a penciled note on her sheet music says "Ally"—squirms, dusts her lap, and frowns at the boys on either side, as if *they* could pull off anything like I've done. Finally, Ally just blinks and falls in a note or two behind everyone else.

I step out of the row, slide back against the classroom wall. About forty chairs and as many music stands are set on risers, sloping down to the conductor—the board says Mrs. Marquez—who is waving her arms and talking over the music. There are posters of composers, diagrammed instruments, a smell of wood and brass and body odor. A piano sits to one side. Instrument cases and backpacks are spread everywhere on the floor, under the seats, against the wall by the door.

The piece they play is severely off-key. This is Buckwood Middle, not the Pittsburgh Symphony. But off-key is better than Matt's screaming inside my head.

I edge the wall as the band runs through the piece from top to bottom without a stop. Matt has a trumpet solo. I wasn't the musical twin, so I don't know for sure, and it's only a few seconds long, but it sounds like he's hitting all the right notes. I look at my ghostly fingers and wonder what it would have been like to have had the lessons he's had—but what's the use of that?

From this angle I'm really able to study Matt's face, which—except for his pimples and my sliced eyebrow—is a clone of my own. Despite the anger and confusion that I know he's feeling, he loves this, loves music. Reading his mind—or rather that whirling thing that is his heart—I sense that besides Trey, and biking by himself, music might be the one thing that gets him through his dark days.

I recall why I'm here. *Get his attention for a moment, then stand aside.*

The piece ends raggedly.

"Hmm . . ." Mrs. Marquez glances at the clock on the wall. "We have a few minutes. Let's run through the middle bars again, and this time when the saxes pull back, Matt, why don't you enter with a big, bright attack on your first note? Knock us off our seats." She smiles.

"Sure," he says, "I like that."

His first note? Big, bright attack?

Thank you, Mrs. Marquez!

She tells them the measure, then counts off. The band starts more or less together and is soon up and swinging. Matt listens, all the while rolling his middle fingers over the buttons the way he seems to like, when Ally and the saxes do their long sweep up.

Matt lifts the trumpet to his lips, fills his cheeks with air, and just as the saxes drop off, I slam my hands down on his fingers as hard as I can. There's no pressure, of course, but if Matt is so obsessed with me, he'll feel something.

Boy does he.

My touch goes through him like a million volts. His

fingers seize up, but—and here's the great part of haunting a trumpet player—he's already pushing two lungfuls of breath into the mouthpiece.

He blows a sound like a cow fart.

Mrs. Marquez jumps and slams back into the whiteboard, the players around him shriek to a stop. One—the joker of the woodwinds—falls to the floor, kicking over his music stand—"You knocked me off my seat!"

Matt is left there holding his trumpet while the rest of the band gags. His face is lobster red, his eyes as wide as moons.

This is the moment I choose to scream inside his head.

"Heyyyyyy, Mattttttttt!"

He jumps to his feet. "Ahhhhh!"

The bell rings, the class collapses, and Matt tears out into the hall.

He tears out into the hall and accidentally bumps a kid lightly with his trumpet case. Matt barrels away, wanting only to be invisible. You wouldn't believe the angry sparks flying off him. They'd cut you.

The kid he bumped into so lightly—who, if he were anywhere near normal, would have let it go—starts shouting at Matt.

"Hey, doofus!"

He sports an upright quiff of red hair and a red face to match his red T-shirt. All that red matches the anger of Matt's sparks.

Now, this kid is in school, he's got good teachers—I saw him sitting in the class with that teacher who didn't give Matt detention—but he's not thinking about learning anything. No, he has to prove himself.

"Hey, get back here!"

Matt moves on, unaware, to his locker. Red tramps after him. When he's near enough, he flicks Matt's hair and snaps his fingers at his ear.

"Leave me alone!" Matt jerks away from the lockers and pushes his way down the hall.

Kids are dumb. They pick on you because your pain makes you different. "You're suffering? Let me make fun of you so you'll feel worse. That's my power." Not even animals think like that.

"Hey, Egan. Your father cuts our lawn. He stinks at it, too!"

Matt goes on his way, and I see in this kid's confused mind that he's thinking of something worse. When he starts with "My dad says your father's a drunk," I focus all my energy and thrust my hand into his neck.

Not *at* his neck. *Into* it.

First, Red stops dead in the hall. Then I wiggle my

fingers around, and he grabs his throat and makes choking noises. He tries to talk, but it's a squeak. He staggers away from Matt, twitching and gasping, and runs down the hall to the water fountain, to the applause of ten or twelve kids whose thoughts tell me he's taunted before.

All in all, a good first haunting.

13

TREY IS TREY IS TREY IS TREY

I hang back while Matt mopes around for the rest of the day. If he sees a pencil, he wants to throw it. After supper, when I watch him bang out the screen door and cut across the lawn into the woods, I know what visitation number two will be.

Him and Trey together.

I'll see what's what between these two.

As you head north into, then out of, the patch of woods on the side and back of our house, you come to a long flat lot between our block and the one behind. It's not quite deep enough to build on, so it's just grass and weeds. The surrounding houses divide the task of mowing—Dad pitched in one summer I remember—making a ridge where the various lawns meet.

I tag after Matt as he crosses the lot to the upper street. It's cooling now, the sun is nearly down. He reaches the northwest corner and takes a right onto Campbell, where he trots diagonally across the street.

I don't have to look, so I just step out after, when this pickup accelerating from the far corner does a sudden squiggle, and brakes, just a tap, as if its driver sees me. Is it the same pickup as this morning? I didn't pay enough attention then, but I do now. It's small and gray, not new, with a vertical dent in the driver's door. I step away to the sidewalk and peer inside the truck as it passes. The driver's a man, I can tell, but he motors off too quickly for me to see his face. It's about seven in the evening, so the sun is low and lying flat on the road.

To materialize, you catch the light and use the dust in the air to take a bit of form. You're like a shaft of thickened air. Maybe I'm so wrapped up in the whole Matt thing, I'm collecting air faster than usual. This will tend to make me more *there* than normal. Even if the pickup driver didn't actually see *me*, he may have noticed a sudden wisp of shadow and reacted.

Matt turns when he hears the truck hit its brakes, but he doesn't slow. He hurries to the next corner, turns right, crosses again, and jumps up the front steps of a two-story factory house more or less like ours. He rings the bell, but that's just a courtesy, because as he does this he tugs on the handle and enters.

I enter too, no handle required.

While Matt's greeting Trey's parents, who welcome him into the living room, I glide up to Trey's room to size it up. Moving is the easiest thing for dead people. You just go where you want.

Trey's bedroom is plain, and Trey is not in it. There are two big windows, dark now, three light green walls, one dark blue. The bed is wedged into a sort of alcove, with a large poster of an old book cover on the wall over the foot of the bed. *Of Mice and Men.* A jammed bookcase stands on the left side of one of the two windows. I look around for stuffed toys, tutus, pennants, bows and arrows, posters of NASCAR drivers or pop stars, male or female. None. Outside of being kind of booky and serious, I can't tell much from the room about Trey's personality.

The door swings wide, and Trey—in jeans and a purple T-shirt with a faded Prince symbol on it—plops on the bed in the middle of maps and papers suspiciously like Matt's.

Two seconds later my brother climbs the stairs. Trey bounces up, smiling, and the zingy thing happens. Calm sparks from Trey. Matt's are sharper, but blue, and coil around Trey's head.

"So . . . ," Trey says, settling back against the pillows while Matt slinks into the desk chair and I squirrel up in the corner. "I've been sort of obsessed with Georgia—"

"Mrs. Marquez taught us that song," Matt says with a sad chuckle.

Trey stares. "Yeah, I don't know what that means."

"'Georgia on My Mind'?" Matt says. "The famous song? Gosh, if it's not Prince, you are musically illiterate."

"Wow, two words, eight syllables. Such a brainiac you are. Look, forgetting that your dad was born in Georgia, you said he was stationed at Fort Benning?"

"He trained there, and his unit or whatever went to Afghanistan."

"What about your mom?"

"She wasn't in the army. Or the marines or navy or air force, either."

"You're on fire tonight. You should do Vegas," Trey deadpans. "Was *she* ever in Georgia? Even for, like, a minute. A layover at the Atlanta airport, maybe? That's a big hub. A hub is what they call the major headquarters for an air—"

"I know what a hub is, you hub." Matt shakes his head. "Nope. No Georgia for Mom. That's been proved. I have it here." He swings his messenger bag into his lap and searches among its contents for the police file. He slips it out, flips through some pages, and reads.

"'Mrs. Egan claims she has never lived in or visited the state of Georgia. Subsequent background checks reveal this to be correct.'" He looks at Trey. "I know zero about when my dad was a kid. He never talks about his past. Maybe there's nothing to learn. I don't know. . . ."

"What's eating you?"

Matt shrugs. "Weird band practice today. Never mind."

Trey chews this over. "Military stuff could be tough to find out, if he's not sharing, but my mom does genealogy, and I could look up when he lived in Georgia. What's his birthday? Middle name?"

"Really?" Matt perks up a little. "April 30, 1979. Robert. Gary Robert Egan."

Trey drags a laptop across the bed and starts typing. "Gary Robert Egan . . . There's a census every decade, they should have some . . ." Trey reads, scrolls, reads more, clicks a couple of times. "And . . . boom—805 East Magnolia Street, Valdosta, Georgia. He's there in 1980. He was a baby. And again in 1990. The house is still there. I'll download a picture of it. Ten years later he's living in Pittsburgh." Trey punches the return key a couple of times, and a printer on the desk slides out several pages.

Matt snatches the sheets with a quivering hand. "This is his house down there? It's tiny. Wow, Dad lived there. Seriously, he never says a word about when he grew up."

"Maybe he made enemies with a neighbor kid. He stole a girl's ball or something, and she grew up and got revenge?"

"Because Georgia has only the one ball?" Matt says. "Trey, you're so weird."

"You're weirder. When was he at Fort Benning?"

"Oh-two. Then Afghanistan a year later."

More clicking. "That was early days in the war. Forty-eight men died in Afghanistan in oh-three. Hard to tell from this if any were from Fort Benning. Here's another printout. You know, sometimes, soldiers get PTSD. Post-traumatic—"

"I know what PTSD is. I don't think my dad has it, but who knows?"

I'm trying to find my moment, but this is all stuff I never knew. On the latest printout is a ridiculously short summary of the Afghan war, and a grid jammed with the totals of American casualties month by month, through seventeen years. I think of warships docking in Port Haven.

"Does he talk about it?" Trey asks. "What happened over there?"

Matt makes a sound halfway between a sigh and a groan. "Not with me. Why the heck don't they just tell me stuff?"

"Parents are all about secrets," Trey says. "Except mine. Man, no secrets at all. Which I guess is maybe good probably. Did you ever think to poke through your mother's secret junk. Maybe she has more police files. Or other clues?"

"I really don't think I'm going to get lucky twice."

Lucky. Yeah. Real lucky.

Seriously, I feel bad, lurking here, knowing the police file, the maps, even this printout, are completely about me, and all I'm doing is gawking. I decide I need to stop the funny business. No more pranks. He's on the edge. But before I'm able to do visitation number two, his phone bings.

He yanks it from his pocket. "Eh. Mom wants me home. For some reason."

Trey glances at the clock on the desk. "It *is* kind of late. Sorry. I know it's tough to be there."

Neither of them moves for, like, two full minutes. I like Trey. I want to appear to Trey the way I'm planning to appear to Matt, and I know I could because of the sparks and because there's so much light coming from Trey. But not yet. *It ain't going to do you no good,* Pink Hair said. I have to get my brother alone first, anyway. And soon.

Matt finally stands, folds the printouts into his bag, opens the door. There's a little hug, then he heads out and down the stairs.

The moon, three-quarters full, is up over the trees. Its light is ghostly pale, making shadows even blacker. It's colder since he left our house. I feel October's breath just around the corner, dying to slide in.

At home we go up the front steps like we did a thousand times together, only this time he doesn't know we're together. He's alone in his mind and in his body. I'm alone too because when Mom opens the door for us she sees only Matt.

Don't be sad or anything. I'm just saying.

Looking at her now, it puzzles me how I can ever appear

to Mom. You need light to appear. There has to be light in the air, so the person can see you, but that person also has to be light inside, to give him or her sight. Mom's got secrets whirling around inside her like a simmering industrial fire. I don't know if there's enough light for me. Which sounds selfish, but isn't meant to be.

As I pass I feel that Mom loves Matt so much that she aches when he's around, but she's terrified he's pulling away because our dad's obsession with my death is rubbing off on him. Since Matt's started to hide his own secrets—which she can totally sense—her love has gone dark, like a switched-off light. I feel all of this oozing from her.

"Homework?" Dad calls from the kitchen. He tries for a kind voice, but he's tired.

"On it." Matt also tries to be bright. "I got what I needed from Trey." Inside his bag are the printouts of Georgia and Afghanistan. "I'm going up. Love you. Love you, Mom."

"Okay," she says, with the stiff smile she gets when he and our dad say more than two words to each other. Her hands tremble when she closes the door. "Love you."

"*Good night, Mom,*" I say. "*Good night, Dad. I'm here, too.*"

The words sound hollow and almost snarky in my mind. My parents can't even guess I'm home and that bothers me. I follow Matt silently upstairs.

His room is dark. He doesn't care, doesn't switch on either the ceiling light or the lamp on the desk or the flashlight he keeps under his pillow. He just plops onto his bed and closes his eyes.

"*Matt.*"

He doesn't respond. Not a flinch.

"*Yo. Matt.*"

Nothing.

Trying to beam a sliver of the moon's glow into his room, I hurl myself at the shade over the window by his desk. The dumb thing doesn't move. I do it again, this time with my fingers clutching at the top roller. Nope.

A third time, now with a running start from out in the hall, straight through his closed door, aiming right at the top of the window and—*bang!*—the shade snaps up.

Matt jumps out of bed. "Geez!"

"You all right up there?" Dad calls up.

"Yeah. Fine!" he yells. "I guess . . ."

His head swivels comically around the room. He freezes when he sees a form take shape in the moonglow from the window—a misty figure sitting cross-legged on his desk in the filmy white light. Me.

He sees.

He stares.

He begins to choke.

14

ME AND MY HALO

"What in holy heck are you?"

Matt's really hoping I don't answer. I mean, he's asking the question, but no way does he want a reply. I give him one anyway.

"Obi-Wan Kenobi. Your only hope."

I say this in his mind, which Russell insists is how you have to start when you haunt people. For, like, a minute, his mouth hangs open, with little strings of spit from the top lip to the bottom. He can't make out my face yet, but he sees something.

"Well, get out of here!" He scrabbles back against the wall as far as he can. "Just get out!"

"Matt?" Mom calls.

"You begged me to come. You screamed for me to come."

Matt's response is simple. "No. I didn't." His voice is pitched very high. "I'm okay," he calls down.

"You're kinda not," I say, moving from inside voice to outside voice, to see if he hears. He blinks at that, so I know he hears me. "I'm Denis, by the way."

"You're n-n-not Denis."

"Uh-huh, I am. Aren't you glad to see me? You'd better be. I went through so much weird junk to get here, you don't want to know. But I'll tell you anyway. There's this giant, hot razor. . . ."

Matt begins to twitch his head from side to side.

It's so odd, looking at yourself do things you're not doing. Except for the long, messy hair, we're so much alike in the face, the Egan chin, our mannerisms, our quirks. With twins as identical as we are—were—it's crazy seeing yourself, but not you. Like gazing into a mirror where your reflection is doing things you're not.

"I'm getting out of here." He steps to the door.

I really don't want to break the spell, but I fly into his path and try to hold the light with me. This is important. First, you catch the light, then you keep it. Apparently I'm good at this, because I manage to block the door.

"Seriously, bro? You don't recognize your own brother?

I'm Denis. Denis Egan, your brother. Your *twin*."

He backs up to the wall at the foot of his bed and tries again with a simple, "No."

"But yes. Denis. Me. Twin. You've been screaming at me for days, and I'm here to tell you to knock it off. It's messing with my beauty death."

"You are some kind of freak."

"You are."

"Denis is dead."

"No, really?"

"You're not here."

"I sort of am," I say.

"I can't even see your face. There's light glaring behind your head."

"There's always light behind my head, bro. I'm holy. Wait. No, I'm not. But the light, that's my thing."

"Well, switch it off. It's annoying."

Matt's trying to get control of himself by being aggressive, which Russell says is a standard response to haunting. Still, I allow the light to drain off slowly enough for him to make out my features—his features. I'm not in moonlight anymore, and the brilliance has dimmed, but I'm still visible to him. GeeGee would be so proud.

Matt rattles his head like his ears are filled with water. "You're lying. You can't be Denis."

"Look. My eyebrow. See?"

"He always had that, but you're not him, because Denis died when he was seven years old. You look . . . you look as old as me."

"Thanks to you, I do."

"Why are you twelve? If you really *are* Denis, *who died five years ago*, how did you get as old as me?"

"Ah. I have a theory about that."

He blinks in my direction. "You have a . . ."

"You see—and stop me if you've heard this before—I aged because you kept imagining me doing things *with you as you aged*. Get it? You'd think of me biking around with you, playing ball, swimming, studying, joking, playing video games, all of it. You needed a playmate, and you kept wanting it to be me. Memories are a big deal where I come from. That's how I got older along with you."

"Uh-huh."

"This doesn't always happen, of course," I add. "There's this girl—you don't know her, she's dead—but her name's Ellen. Well, we call her that. Or Ella, maybe. Either. She's got a funny ponytail and sits on the beach every day, watching the boats come in. For the last thirteen years she's been exactly seven years and ten months old. How do I know? Russell told me. He's a guy up there. Seven years and ten months! For thirteen years! She was basically my age when she got there, but now I'm older than her. Why doesn't *she* get older? I bet you could tell me, but I'll tell you. Russell says that her family keeps remembering her being seven years old. If there are any photos of her, they're when she was seven, and that's all they know, so she stays seven. Dude, it's because of you that I'm twelve, thank you very much. . . ."

His eyes are glazing over.

"But I see I'm losing you. Anyway, I came to tell you to back off with the scratching and the moaning and groaning. Things are okay where I am now. I'm okay. Happy and happy. You don't need to worry about me. Really. It's always sunny. I have a porch. There's water, a beach, all sorts of folks in Port Haven, the part of the afterlife I'm in—"

"You were killed!"

"Says you."

"Says me? Says the world! You know this! You were murdered. It was horrible! There are tons of questions. You can answer them. If you're a ghost, you have to know everything!"

"That's where you're wrong, Captain. I don't know a single thing about how I died. Well, a bridge and/or bridges. Something silver. A spoon maybe. And some tall thing in the corner of my eye that might be a telephone pole. Or the Eiffel Tower. Maybe I died in Paris, that'd be cool—"

"Stop it! You know how you died and who killed you!"

"Sorry. Big blank there. But I have to ask. Why are you all about this now? After five years? Because you finally read the police file?"

"You saw that?"

"I was leaning over your shoulder."

He gives me a face like I stink. "I was seven when you died. I'm twelve now. I was afraid to know before. I'm still afraid, but I need to know. There are hundreds of questions we don't have answers to."

"Except I died. There's no question about that. I'd like to help, but I can't. It's too messy down here, and I need to be the opposite of messy. Plus, I'm dealing with my own junk right now. There's GeeGee slipping away—she's our great-grandmother, by the way—not to mention how I've got to concentrate on my own tiny story fading more each day."

"It's not tiny," he says, pushing strands of loose hair behind his ears. "It's not tiny and it has everything to do with everything!" He wants to say more, but he's suddenly out of breath.

"Look, I have to go back," I tell him. "Really. I *have* to. Besides, there's a party at the beach club tonight. Well, there's a party every night—"

"You're *not* going back! And stop being such a snot about it." He swings out to grab me, clutching nothing but light. He drops his hand.

"I mean it. When you . . . died . . . everything changed. Except no, it didn't change then. It was already changing. You died because of things that were moving years ago. The police file is one thing, but Mom and Dad have secrets they won't tell me. Maybe not even to each other. There's stuff to know. And everything that's happened, our family falling apart, everything that happens every day, all of it, is tied to what happened to you."

I try to take that in. It's too huge to comprehend, so I try to be funny, with an edge.

"Well, I'm sorry I screwed things up. Me dying is so about you."

"I don't mean that!"

Which, of course, I knew, but he storms around the room, then plops back onto the bed because that's where he can see me the best. "Do you know how many times I tried to undo that day, make your death not happen? I went through everything I did, then everything I *ever* did, to understand how if I changed one little thing, I could make you still be alive. Do you know what that's like? I was sure *I* killed you. Mom and Dad, too. We beat ourselves up over and over."

His face is down, his hands covering it. Matt begins to cry.

It's hard to look at him. I imagine him trying to bring me back to life, and I feel like a cheat, a creep, soulless. I try to tell him, but there are no words for it. "You didn't kill me. You didn't."

"Too late now!" he growls, then sniffs up his tears. "Look, I don't know how, but it's not like somebody *randomly* murdered you. Mom and Dad have secrets they probably don't even know they're hiding."

"Matt, I've got nothing for you. We forget our deaths first thing."

"But . . . why? That's so dumb. Why?"

I laugh, but it's a false laugh and I know it. "To scrub yourself clean. That's what death is. You die, you land in Port Haven, and you forget everything from the most recent to the early stuff. Being a baby, growing up with you *always* around—I can still remember that. Biking? Geez, the biking. We went everywhere, didn't we? The time we crashed our bikes head-on, the road trips in the back seat, that spelling game we did with the letters, what was it called?"

"Who cares?" He rubs his palms into his eyes then down his cheeks.

My throat thickens in a way I didn't think possible. I don't even have a throat, not a real one, but it's choking me. "Look, Gettysburg? That's a stunner. It must have been pretty sensational."

He looks up at me with wet eyes. "It was horrible. The searching? Dad's whole crew went down there to the amusement park. Teachers from school. *Your* teachers. The PTA. Everybody. How do you think it was? You were seven and somebody murdered you! It was like it was always raining. All the water, everybody sobbing and yelling. How do you think it was . . ."

The recitation burns my chest. "Matt, I'm so sorry—"

"Don't tell me you're sorry!" he snaps, throwing me an

angry look. "I'm serious. You need to stay until we find out why you were ripped away from us."

"I *can't* stay here. One time through the razor maybe I can survive. It hurts, but I'll make it."

"There's a reason they found you at Gettysburg, you know," he says. "I don't know if it's payback or what, but there's a reason, and it's about you and me and our parents. I need you here, Denis."

"Matt—"

"Haunt me, Denis. *Haunt me!*"

15

BROTHERS

"Haunt you."

Even saying the words aloud, I feel the razor slice into my face. I can barely hold the light.

"Matt, really, I can't do this. . . ."

"Mom started to take your stuff out of our room. Did you know that?"

I didn't.

"After about a year. Your clothes first, then your toys and books. One day she came in and said she wanted to take your bed out, to let me have the whole room to myself. That was the big thing she saved for last."

While he lets that sink in, I look at my bed, not a wrinkle

in the blanket, not a dent in the pillow. "So why is it still here?"

"Dad said wait. He looked at me, but he said it to her. Let it wait. So Mom waited. The bed stayed. It's been here every day since you died."

"Did you even change the sheets? It's got Star Wars sheets on it."

"She made the bed for when you came back, before we knew you wouldn't. A few months later she said let's move to a different house, maybe a different town, but Dad said not yet. Then she wanted a new baby and started fixing up the extra room as a nursery. She said it would help us heal. But he said we're still recovering, no brothers or sisters yet. Okay, she said, but maybe I could have the spare room? I told her no."

It stuns me to imagine five years of Matt and our parents, a family of three that used to be four. What were the days like? The mornings? When they woke up, did it take time to remember I wasn't there anymore? What happened to *me* in their minds? Where did I go?

"After that Mom started to shut down, like *click, click, click*, the lights going off. I didn't want to be like Dad—against her—I just didn't want to leave our room. I couldn't do it. You're right. I still thought of us having fun together. If all your stuff was gone, what would I do?"

My heart aches just looking at his face. "What about Trey?"

"I didn't know Trey yet. And Trey's Trey, but you're my brother."

Matt goes quiet and seems to be trying to come up with more words to explain things, but he doesn't have to. I get it. I feel it.

There's a brand-new laptop sitting on his desk, a birthday present maybe. The box it came in is on the floor next to the desk. The packing foam and empty plastic are stuffed in his wastebasket. At the foot of the bed is not just a student trumpet but a professional one. The phone he uses mainly to call Trey is new too.

He deserves it all, don't get me wrong. It's just that the things our parents would have had to split between us, he's gotten for himself, an only child now. I sense it's Mom who really pushes for these things. Maybe that's how she's able to show she loves him. I think she always figured Matt was her baby and I was Dad's, the way he flew me around the room while she cuddled Matt on her chest. She always hugged him more, loved him more. I'm not judging, just saying that Matt gets great stuff since I'm not here to need any.

That's why when Matt says no to her, it hurts so much.

"Matt, look, I seriously don't remember. Yellow leaves. A dark pole of some kind. Something silver. Snow, maybe, or junk moving in the air?"

He looks up suddenly. "The first snow came the day you died."

"Maybe not snow. Maybe ash from a fire. Confetti from a parade. See? I don't even know what I know."

"So help me find out! I can't do it alone, but *we* could together. Mom and Dad are going down the toilet. *I'm* going down the toilet. You're the only one who can stop it. I need you. We all need you."

This hits me harder than I would have thought. I want to explain death to him, how the razor will cut deeper each time I go through it. I want to tell him I'm afraid my death will be ruined because I'll be too soiled to move on. But why would he even care how much it hurts me?

He's hurting so much more.

"Well," I start. "I mean . . ."

"You mean *what*?"

My head spins. Nothing comes to me fast enough.

He throws up his hands. "Exactly. You're haunting me. Starting now!"

16

GEEGEE'S ADVICE

Well, that was a big fail.

I had just split myself down the middle to tell Matt to leave me the heck alone, and instead I'd vowed to return *and* promised to save my family—if such a thing like saving living people is even possible for a ghost!

I told Matt I needed to talk to GeeGee right away. I had to know how much I can haunt him before it backfires bigtime on me. The razor damage. "Rip, rip, rip!" All of it.

I tear myself from the blade and stagger down the hills. The pain slashes my face, and the long cut burns. I feel like I'm leaving something—a lung or two—back in Matt's world. The hurt fades a little when I finally see GeeGee standing on the flagstone path in front of her house.

"GeeGee!"

She's frowning at the flower bed that runs along the inside of her fence. She's wearing a blue beret, as if she's going out, but she's still in her bathrobe, which is hanging loose. She's also barefoot, her little white feet reminding me of my single bare foot resting on the grass beneath the monument. She smells more like oranges than usual.

"GeeGee?"

She doesn't hear me, doesn't move. I'm not sure exactly what she's looking at, or if she's looking at anything in particular.

I touch her arm. "GeeGee."

"I came downstairs without my feet this morning," she says apologetically, and I wonder if she knows it's me.

"You have your feet, GeeGee," I say, "but you left your shoes inside." I cinch up her bathrobe.

"That's what I mean!" she snaps. "My . . . my . . ."

My chest thrums. "GeeGee, are you all right? Maybe we should go back inside?"

She looks up at me, confused, gives a little shake of her head, then smiles. "Of course." I take her by the arm and we walk up the steps and in, settling in the kitchen. I pour her a glass of water. She doesn't need to drink water; nobody here eats or drinks, it's the idea of it. She takes the glass because I offer it. After a few swallows she pats my hand and appears to see me for the first time.

"Denis, yes? Are you feeling better now? No fever?"

"Am I feeling better? Are you?"

"Oh, yes, yes. You give me myself back. You *revive* me." She pronounces the word carefully, as if it has special meaning for souls, and I make a mental note to ask Russell if it does.

Revive.

Then she breathes in, settles her shoulders, and smiles at me. "There. Better. So. How did it go? Apart from the razor. You don't have to share any details about that, thank you very much!"

GeeGee seems almost back to normal, a sparkle in her eyes that disappears when she sighs.

"The problem is my brother, Matt. He's killing the death out of me."

She seems ready to smile at the joke, but doesn't. I explain my visitations, thinking she'll get a kick out of band practice and the red-haired kid's neck, but I'm not sure she's following what I'm saying. I fill a pot of water for tea.

"There's twisted stuff in our parents' minds, GeeGee. They have secrets. They kept police records from Matt, which is just the tip of the iceberg. There's a lot more they won't talk about."

"It's terrible for a mother to bury a son," she says softly. "You can only hope to see him later. Families are so hard to keep together, you know. So hard . . ."

Sitting quietly at the table, I feel a draft of cold air, and sense that things are happening to GeeGee because everyone who should be remembering her isn't. If it were up to me, she would stay here forever. I know she wants to. I'd be nothing and know no one at all, if not for her.

"I guess they're grieving," I say. "Matt too. Do you remember my father?"

"Your father?" She perks up. "Of course. I believe his name was Gary."

"That's right. Gary Egan. He's your grandson."

"My husband was an engineer named Gary Egan, too. He built factories and coal mines, tunnels and bridges. Some people ask me, why did I go back to my maiden name? My sons, one of them was different. He used it. At the end I used it too. I'm not sorry. Twins run in the family, you know. Alcohol runs in families, too. Your grandfather was a troubled man. He and your father never got along. Gary's mother died of smoking."

"Is my grandfather alive? Dad never talks about him. Joseph Egan. Is he up here?"

Her look turns blank. "I visited, you know. People down there. Him. Others. Too often, perhaps. The razor."

"You visited your son, my grandfather?"

"Oh, how he treated his poor brother. I loved Richard. He was different. Brothers can be so very different. Gary died in Florida on a bridge, did you know that? My husband.

That's why it was so sad, because he built bridges. Gary loved them, as a boy, too."

It's confusing, not helped by the fact that both my dad and GeeGee's husband were named Gary. "Are you saying my great-grandfather built bridges? I think about bridges a lot."

"Oh, dozens of them. Gary died when Gary was in school. I raised him, your father. *His* father kicked him out."

"My dad lived with you?"

"In that tiny house. No lawn, no garage, but I think he liked it. At first, he did. Later there was that awful day he went back. The school bus. And the leg, of course. Well, that changed things."

"Leg? GeeGee? What leg?"

"Now, *my* grandfather Byatt was a soldier, you know. The 13th Pennsylvania Reserves. He lost one at Gettysburg. His right one, I think. Or his left. Leg, I mean."

"*Gettysburg?* They found me at Gettysburg!"

And all at once I feel the threads pull a little tighter and begin to hum.

"They called the Reserves the Bucktails. They were at the Wheatfield. I have a photo of him right up"—she looks at the blank wall next to us—"somewhere. Your father loved that photo. Always posing like Byatt. 'No posing,' I'd say. Gary was obsessed with the Civil War. Maybe that's why he joined the service. Then after all that, the leg."

"What leg, GeeGee? You're talking about my dad now? I know he was in Afghanistan. Is that what you mean? Did something bad happen there?"

"How could it not be bad?"

She says this, fussing with her hands as if wiping crumbs from the front of her robe. I tell her about what I saw in Buckwood and she startles me. "Matt is right. You should haunt him. It *is* your fault your family is broken. You should do whatever you can to stop them flying apart."

I don't like her telling me this. "I told Matt I can't do much. There are clues about my death, though. Weird little things."

GeeGee searches my face for a few seconds. "You could start at the end, see what's there. Work back. It's what they do in mystery stories. Start at the crime scene."

I conjure the images in the police file. "Are you saying follow the evidence?"

"You'll be the detective in your own mystery." She smiles a sliver of a smile, then dabs her old finger on my cleft eyebrow. "I don't remember you getting this."

"I've always had it. It must have been after you . . . you know . . . came here."

She turns her face from me, scanning her kitchen for something familiar but not finding it. "Oh, you wear me out. It's been a long day."

It's midmorning. Not even noon.

GeeGee blinks at her teacup. Her hair is as thin as threads over her skull. When she looks up she seems surprised I'm there. "Maybe you should go now." She falters to stand, and I help her. "You wear me out. I have to rest." Her eyelids flutter as she shuffles from the kitchen to the front door. "Be careful on the stairs. They're steep. Well, you know that."

"Okay, GeeGee. I'll try to get to Gettysburg with Matt. Work backward like you said."

She puts her hand shakily on the door handle. "You're a good young boy. I'm not quite sure who you are, but I love you. I think I do. I'll let you know if I remember any more."

A little chunk of my heart falls off. "I love you, too, Gee-Gee."

"If that's all, then . . ." She opens the door with her slender fingers, then retreats into the house. As I step down the stairs, she quietly closes the door behind her.

17

THE HURT OF NIGHT

The walk outside her house is bright in the full sun. Her lawn, recently trimmed and edged, is the color of a fresh lime. The hydrangeas in the border are blooming full blue, lolling in the breeze from the shore.

Be careful on the stairs, she told me. But her stairs are shallow, like all the stairs here, designed for the elderly. I want to batter down the door, run back in to her, but I don't.

"Matt needs me now, GeeGee. Have a good rest."

I climb away from her house to the hard room at the foot of the hills, where the razor seems more vicious than before. As if the blade knew that my previous visit was my first, it seems doubly angry with me. Does it hurt more to slice multiple times along the same line? Maybe the razor's made that way. I try to shake off the pain, but the cut line burns me all the way through.

Time must be different between the worlds. It's still morning in Port Haven, but it's dark on my street in Buckwood. Night cools the pavement. The blue of the trees to the north seems to wash over our neighborhood. As the lights in my house go off one by one, I think of the porch lamp lit for three solid days before it was turned off. Soon everyone will be asleep or just staring into the dark, trying to calm their hearts.

An engine shifts gears, drives away.

It takes me an instant before I look. Was it the pickup I've seen twice already? Is someone spying on my family? Does the driver notice me?

The street is already empty. The night goes still.

I turn to the house again. Mom's car is gone. Dad's is parked at the top of the driveway. There is sadness rumbling inside the rooms. Steeling myself, I float up the front path and peer inside the window by the door.

The TV flickers in the living room. Dad is sitting alone in front of it, maybe asleep. I shimmer upward and enter the house through Matt's window. His light is on, but he's not there. Something slides across the attic floor above me. I ooze up through the ceiling and find Matt crouching over an old suitcase.

I don't want to be funny, I really don't, but what would you do if you had the chance? I wait until he starts fiddling with the lock, then I scream.

"*Stop! Thief!*"

"Holy crow!" he gasps as he rolls back on his feet. "You idiot! You're insane!"

"Maybe," I reply. "But you asked me to haunt you."

"It's been three days!" he hisses under his breath. "Where have you been? I thought I dreamed you up!"

"Three days? Bro, I'm sorry. I don't know what happened. I was only there for minutes."

"Heaven should get a clock. Now, clam up. I don't want Dad to hear me."

"He's sleeping in front of some show."

"And I waited forever for him to do that." Matt breathes deep to calm himself. "This is Mom's old suitcase. Trey gave me the idea to look for her stuff. Mom keeps it buried up here."

He twitches the paper clip in the lock, stops, then catches me in the flashlight. "Wait. You can't get this open, can you?"

"Sorry. I'm not Houdini. I'm just dead like him. And taller. Did you know he was short? He's short."

He grumbles and fiddles again. But it's an old suitcase with an old lock, and soon—*click*—it's open. Setting the suitcase down, he lifts the lid, then groans again. "Clothes." He holds up a fancy pink sweater with pearls sewn into the neckline.

"Mom never wore that," I whisper. "She's not a pink person."

"Maybe she used to be, before . . . everything."

Which might be a dig at my selfish death, but I let it go. There are a couple of blouses; skinny lady belts wound in coils and tied with ribbons; several folded scarves; and two, no three, berets in different shades of blue.

"This might be GeeGee's stuff," I say. "She wears berets. Sometimes. She had one on . . . before."

It's only after Matt lifts the clothes away that we see something else. A silver-framed photograph from the nineteenth century, the kind that have an odd silvery sheen. It's a young man in an old uniform, staring grim faced into the lens, a long barreled musket at his side.

"Is this from the Civil War?" I whisper. "GeeGee told me about him. Her grandfather or someone. Bryan? B-something. I forget. He fought at, guess where, Gettysburg. Plus, our dad was all about the Civil War when he was young. I bet this is GeeGee's stuff from when he lived with her."

"Which probably means something I have no idea of," he says, mangling the language.

Scrabbling through the rest of the stuff, Matt finds another photograph. A snapshot of a white farmhouse surrounded by fields, with rolling green hills in the background.

"Familiar?" he asks me.

"No."

"Really?"

"Yeah, why?"

"Ghosts don't actually know very much, do they? First, how to tell time. Now this."

"Just keep looking."

Next is a stack of bad kid artwork. A drawing I see as a green balloon on a string Matt insists is a tree with a skinny trunk. Pages of turkeys made from small painted handprints.

"These are our hands. Look at the dates," Matt whispers, holding the flashlight close. "They're from when we were . . . two. Mom keeps them hidden up here?"

"You're not suggesting they should be framed?"

"Well, mine."

Tons more artwork made out of construction paper, caked with thick gobs of paste. Suns with squiggly beams. Nightmare houses where no line is straight. Finally, tucked into a satin pocket at the very bottom of the suitcase, is an envelope of doctors' records. Matt sifts through them.

"The usual checkups at the doctor we must have had as kids. Sore throats, ear infections, antibiotics, bee-stings."

There is a stack of vaccination records. He flips through several identical cards.

"You start getting flu shots when you're one," he says, like he's an expert, "then every year for a few years—"

"Wait, go back," I say. "There. That one. It's different. The stamp on it reads . . . 'Armstrong County Health

Department, Kittanning.' The others are stamped Lawrence County. Buckwood is in Lawrence. What were we doing in Kittanning?"

Matt focuses on the signature and date. "October twenty-ninth. Dr. Vishna-something."

"Fine, but why did we get vaccinations in Buckwood every year except that one? We got all the others here. Why not when we were two?"

"Whoa, Sherlock," he says. "Maybe we were traveling when we needed them?"

I try to swat him. I fail. "Except you *schedule* vaccinations. You don't get vaccinations when you're driving through strange places."

The two forms—Matt's and mine—are so unspecific. Our names, the date, a couple of check marks, Dr. V's flowery signature.

I keep working at it. "Unless . . . unless you're there for a while. Unless you're staying there. Where is Kittanning anyway? You're all about maps."

"I don't know—"

"Matt? Are you on the phone?" Dad growls from the foot of the stairs. "Why aren't you in bed?"

We freeze. Of course I don't really have to, but I do anyway.

"In a minute, Dad!" Matt calls back. "Sorry!" He quickly shoves everything back into the suitcase, scurries down to his room, and leaps into his bed. "Okay, so Armstrong County? Why were we there when we were two, and for how long? I'll put Trey on the case."

"Trey, huh? You really like Trey, don't you?"

"What are you, still seven?"

I try to come up with something snarky, but it stings to hear Matt's comment, so I don't. "Anyway, the real reason I came back from Port Haven is to tell you I have a plan."

Matt sits up on his elbows. "A plan to solve your murder?"

"Uh-huh. We—you—*we*—need to follow everything we know, all the clues, from Gettysburg back to the beginning. GeeGee told me that's how you do it. It's the only way to get the big picture and the only way to put me to rest."

"Meaning?"

"Tell them to drive you to Gettysburg."

"You *are* insane. Mom will completely freak if I so much as *mention* the Civil War. The war between the states, brother versus brother, it all equals Denis, Denis, Denis. She's sick to death of your death."

"Then Dad. Just you and him go. And invisible me, of course. I could find out stuff you can't, then tell you. You'll seem like the genius I am."

Matt is quiet for a while. "Seriously, if we could end this thing, Mom and Dad might be human again. You'll appear to them?"

"I can't spread me around. You can tell Trey, but no one else."

He laughs. "Oh, I already told Trey. How could I not?"

I half expected this. "Fine, but just Trey. Oh, and I almost forgot, someone's watching you."

"From above?"

"From a truck. I've seen it around a few times. Maybe it's that red-haired kid's father, waiting to get revenge for the throat thing."

"His name is John Foley, and that's on you."

"I'm just saying. A gray pickup."

"Perfect. I'm being stalked. That's all I need."

"Ask Dad tomorrow about Gettysburg. And don't forget to get Trey working on Kittanning."

Matt rests his head on his pillow. "Now I'll never sleep."

18

THE BIG ASK

Because time seems messed up between Port Haven and here, I stick around while Matt grinds through a ton of words in his head, a real gravel soup, for the best way to ask to see where they found my body. Every time he seems ready to, he chickens out because, for Mom, *Gettysburg* is practically a swear word, and even thinking it proves that Matt is betraying her.

Trey's advised him to "ask your dad when it's just the two of you," but Matt's convinced that if Mom's present when he brings it up, it won't be half as bad as if he and Dad conspire between themselves, then spring it on her.

I back away from the debate, but maybe not far enough.

• • •

Wednesday night at dinner, they're sitting around the table. This is ground zero for heavy discussions and, honestly, I don't like the place anymore. I used to, lots, but there are only three chairs since Mom took mine away. Who am I to complain, except, you know, it was my chair. . . .

Anyway, they talk about school, fire drills in the rain, the dozens of new plantings, and the five temporary classroom trailers Dad helped put in because two elementary schools merged because Buckwood's population is dropping because jobs are drying up because stores are closing because natural gas drilling because international because because because.

Mom mentions the thunderstorm forecast for tonight and wonders if "we should run and close all the windows after supper," and Matt says, "I will," then there's a sudden gap in the talk, and he puts down his fork.

"I was thinking . . . ," he starts, but stops when Mom flicks her eyebrows up at him. The way she does it— so instantly— shows she's been waiting for a challenge, and here it is, as if she's saying, *Now what?* Mom is on such a short fuse, Matt considers bailing out, but he sees me lurking in the doorway and goes on. "I was thinking I'd like to go to Gettysburg."

"Good for you," I tell him. *"Throw it right out there."*

Mom flinches and springs back in her chair. "What? Oh no, Matt. You don't want to do that. It's so sad there. It's a terrible place. For us. No. Please, no."

"I get it, but—"

"They're all terrible, battlefields. You think they're beautiful, rolling hills and trees, then you learn how many people died so horribly there. No, Matt. No."

"But it's almost five years and I've never been." Matt says this without emotion, trying to keep a lid on what he must know will happen next.

"No, no." Mom sounds almost strangled. "Gary, you don't think it's a good idea, do you?" She looks at Dad. No, she *glares* at him. Matt has just conjured a thicket of tension in the kitchen, and everything stops.

Dad doesn't answer.

"Do you? *Gary?*"

He keeps his head down over his plate, breathing in and out, his broad shoulders moving, his hands not moving, one of which is holding his knife just above his plate. Mom must know he's been there by himself, often, since I died. She shifts her weight in her chair and dares him again.

"Gary, *do* you?"

"You know what, I'm fine," Matt says, as if he's been told there's no more soup. "It's just an idea. No big deal."

Mom and Dad both relax a fraction, but only a fraction. Mom hovers over her food again, pokes it around, starts picking slowly.

"But I *was* interested in, you know, Georgia," Matt says. "Dad, I know you're from there, but we've never gone."

"Holy cow, Matt!" Mom's cutlery clicks on her plate.

"Georgia," Dad says, his first word for minutes.

"Yeah," Matt gulps. "There's a boy from Savannah in our class. I think he's from there. He told us, well, he did a report, that it's really nice there. Beaches and stuff. You were born in Georgia, right? Your folks?" He wants this to hang in the air for a little bit, but Mom won't let it.

"Really, Matt?" she says. "First Gettysburg, now Valdosta? From bad to worse? Or, I don't know which is worse. For crying out loud, that was another war, wasn't it? And nobody won that one! Matt, please don't ask Daddy about his fa—family. Can we talk about something else?"

"No, it's okay," Dad says.

"Is it?" Mom shoves her chair back a few inches. "Is it okay? Really? You're going to tell your son about your father and the bus and the leg? It's closed. Gary, please."

The leg? What the heck?

Dad shakes his head. "Not about that—"

"Well, I can't hear any of it again." She kicks back from the table again and stands. "Gary, you moan about it at night at least once a week. Reliving it all at the table is not going to do any good, certainly not for me. I love you, Gary, and you, Matt, of course I do, I just can't hear it. Go ahead. Tell him. Tell your son every bloody detail. Excuse me."

Mom reels away from the table and storms out of the kitchen. Seconds later, you can hear the jingle of keys, a door slam, and the car start. She backs out of the driveway.

Somebody honks. She honks back. Two engines roar away in different directions. I look out. Was it the pickup? I'm too late to see. The kitchen is now a cauldron. Dad hangs his head, bobbing it as fast as his heart is beating.

"I'm sorry," Matt says, his eyes tearing up. "I didn't know. . . . I'm really sorry, Dad. We don't have to—"

"When we get to the battlefield, okay? I'll go with you, I'll take you to Gettysburg." Dad's face is gray as stone, cracking as he tries to make it smile. "We'll go soon. If you still want to know about me growing up, I'll tell you there."

19

DRAGGING AWAY

Leaving Mom turns out uglier than ugly.

Matt hasn't breathed the G word for two days, when Dad finally texts him from work Friday morning to say that the two of them will leave Saturday at dawn and maybe stay overnight somewhere. But if Mom asks, Matt's to tell her they'll be back that night.

"We're taking off early," he tells me when I return to his room Friday night. I had been scouting the neighborhood, trying to spot the pickup, but it began to sprinkle. Rain can give me form, and I can't risk being seen.

"Good." I slouch on my bed, not ruffling the covers. "Phase One of the Mystery of Me."

"We stopped taking road trips after you," he says. "And

I can't remember *ever* just being me and Dad together"—his phone rings—"You'll be in the back, I guess, right? Hey, Trey . . ."

In the back. The words jangle. I don't know why they do, but a second later, they're gone. It doesn't go anywhere.

"I'm putting it on speaker so Denis can hear."

Trey whispers from the phone. "D-Denis? Are you really there? In Matt's room?"

I realize that this is the first time Trey knows I'm there. "Tell Trey, hey."

Matt says, "He says 'hey.' Which gives you an idea of his vocab."

"Wow. I have chills," Trey says. "Seriously, chills."

"Calm your jets. He's not all *that* cool," Matt says, grinning at me. "So what'd you find?"

Trey adjusts. "Okay. So. Kittanning, where you got your two-year-old vaccinations, is east of us about an hour. I searched *Egan,* but no census results in your family. One of the first things that pops up is the county jail nearby. I hope that's not why you were there."

Matt manages a laugh. "I don't think they lock up two-year-olds—"

"I *mean,* that you were there to be *close* to the jail."

"*Because* . . . Dad *was* inside?" I say.

Matt shakes his head. "I'm pretty sure we'd know that."

"Know what?" Trey asks.

"If our dad was in jail. They keep secrets, but they couldn't keep *that* secret, could they? Still, they are a secret society, them. Georgia. The bus. Vaccinations. Some leg."

Trey goes on. "Otherwise, it's just a place people live, like anywhere. Oh, except there was a big coal miners' strike in 1910. Sixteen miners and police died. There are folk songs about it."

Matt squints into the air. "Relevance?"

"Probably none. Still searching. Bye, Denis!"

After Trey hangs up, I try to digest this. "It's not much, but the jail might explain the guy following us. You know, Dad's cellmate."

"What, after ten years? You've been watching too much TV."

"We don't have TVs in Port Haven. Although, we'd make a great show. The characters we have! Anyway, are you all ready to slip out the door before Mom gets up?"

He groans. "She's not happy. Be grateful you don't have to live with the fallout."

I give him the eye. "Is that a dead-brother joke?"

"No. It's an Egan joke. She hates that we're going in the first place. She'll explode if we take more than a day."

As it happens, the plan to leave early misfires. It pours buckets during the small hours of Saturday morning—the third stormy night this week. Mom wakes Dad to run and close the windows so the rain won't come in. Except that jumping from window to window agitates him so much, when he finally nods off an hour later, he oversleeps.

When Matt hears Dad moving around in the morning, he tiptoes downstairs with his bag, only to find Mom in the kitchen, brewing coffee and cooking breakfast.

He guesses right away that this is to get them back for going to Gettysburg.

"Hi, Mom." He drops his bag in the back hall. "Crazy rain, huh?"

She slides his plate down at an angle, pulls her hand away, doesn't meet his look, doesn't speak.

"It woke me up twice," Matt adds quietly.

Dad comes down a few minutes later and gets his plate delivered the same way. Mom doesn't sit at the table herself, but goes into the bathroom off the kitchen, and puts the fan on. I'm thinking she can't bring herself to simply bolt back upstairs, leaving them alone, but she doesn't want to talk to them either.

"You all set?" Dad asks Matt.

Matt nods. "I have my stuff, maps, and books. The battle was the turning point of the war. The first three days of July 1863 were so hot . . ."

He stops when Mom opens the bathroom door abruptly. She shoots a look, not at either of them, but at the plates, then whips the messy table clean, before they've finished eating.

Dad storms out and throws his gear into the car, not saying two words to Mom because she won't say two words to him.

"Bye, Mom," Matt says at the door.

Seeing her like that, not hugging him good-bye, not touching him, not even looking at him, Matt chokes. Just when you'd think she'd melt and pull him into her arms, she doesn't. She faces the counter and stares out the window to the backyard. She's shaking, but she won't turn.

"Bye, Mom," Matt repeats.

No response.

"Mom, go to him!"

Matt hears what I say, but she doesn't.

Then, as he goes to close the door behind him, she quickly whirls around, and in two steps is holding him. "Be careful, be careful, I love you."

"I love you, too, Mom. Just . . . I want to see it, that's all. We'll be back tonight."

She doesn't sense that this is two lies in one. He doesn't *just* want to see Gettysburg, and he might *not* be back tonight.

"Come on, Matt!" Dad yells from the car. "We have to roll to have any time at the battlefield before heading home."

And seconds later, just before seven o'clock, we pull out of the driveway, with me tucked invisibly into the back seat.

20

THE UNFINAL RESTING PLACE

Gettysburg is a long, low scoop east across the state from Buckwood. It's quiet in the car. I leave Matt alone with his hot, churning thoughts, his spurts of sparks. Somewhere in midstate, I whisper in his head that I'm sorry again about the mess I made when I died, but he doesn't answer.

About an hour outside Gettysburg we start seeing signs for the "military park," the tourist way of saying "battlefield." Matt drags his messenger bag from the floor behind his seat. Maps, books, brochures—not the newspapers or photos of me from the police file of course, though that's what he wishes he could look at. He unfolds the battlefield map against the dashboard.

"It was near a monument?" Matt says quietly, pretending

to be searching the location symbols. "Where they found Denis?"

Dad glances over and taps the spot Matt knows so well. "Georgia."

"Right." Matt pulls out a guide he downloaded and printed from the net. We are streaming along, there's not a lot of traffic. Just when I wonder how he'll play what he already knows against what he needs to hear from Dad, he blurts it out, pretending to have just thought of it.

"Georgia must mean something, right? That Denis was found at the monument of your state? There are so many states here."

Dad keeps his eyes on the road, narrows them, chews the inside of his mouth for a while. He finally shakes his head. "I left there so long ago. I mean, yeah, I trained back at Fort Benning, but those were good guys, all of them. Some were still around five years ago, a few weren't."

Matt shifts his eyes to the back, which is where I am, sitting behind Dad, who's just gone dark, like a connection has been severed.

"*We need to know way more than that,*" I whisper.

But Dad's clammed up and Matt backs off from asking more. Miles of silence. All told, after a couple of stops, including one for a fast-food lunch, we pull into town around eleven thirty.

•   •   •

The Gettysburg National Military Park is vast, over four hundred acres of green meadow, trimmed grass, countless wooden fences and stone walls, stands of tall trees that may or may not have been there during the battle in early July 1863, and winding paved roads that have certainly been laid since. There are tour buses, cars, vans on the battlefield roads, and hikers on paths. Sun shines squarely on the monuments and signs. According to the map that Matt has spread on his knees, the park encircles the town of Gettysburg on three sides like an invading army, mimicking the actual way the armies were deployed in 1863.

We drive east along a rising, angled road called Millerstown Road. At a point that looks like any other, Dad pulls the car onto the grass by a white picket fence and cuts the engine. We overlook a long rising field. Dad gets out. We do too.

"Is this where the Honda was seen?" I ask.

Matt has to wait for Dad to say it. "Dad?"

"The car." Dad sets his hands on his hips. "The stolen car that the police think Denis was . . . brought here in. It was seen parked around this spot, give or take. The monument's over there." Dad points up across the field toward a block of stone sprouting near some cannons.

"I keep imagining someone climbing this fence and carrying Denis and laying him at the monument," Dad says, "and never mind who it was, *why* did he do it. Just *why*? What was the point of it? I mean, sorry, Matt, but I know you've seen enough TV to know that bodies are . . . bodies aren't *placed* around. They're hidden or buried or dumped, and most of the time you never find them. The police told me. So why was Denis left out in such a public place, and why that way? Somebody cleaned the wounds on his foot, for God's sake. . . ."

Dad says this last part in a bare whisper.

I wonder why too. Why all of it.

Matt wipes his nose. His eyes are damp. They found his twin brother's lifeless body so near to where he's standing, and he's struggling not to cry.

"I want to see the place," he says softly. "The monument."

"Do you think you're ready?"

Matt nods once.

After one last quiet look, we drive up the gentle incline to the corner of West Confederate Avenue. There are signs for the Peach Orchard and the Wheatfield, where GeeGee said her grandfather fought—places that might sound peaceful but whose ground is soaked in blood. We don't follow those signs, but turn right at the corner, past an observation building that Dad calls Longstreet Tower. A parking lot sits below it on the left.

We back in and sit in the car.

Matt cracks his window to let air in. The monument is across the road not two hundred paces from where we sit. Some yards beyond is a low, wandering wall of piled stones above a dip in the sloping land. Seeing the memorial, my gravestone at the top of a wide field, I feel sick.

I didn't die here, but I was placed to rest here. I was posed with the care of an undertaker, against the memorial's base in a sitting position, waiting for someone to find and decode me.

We get out and walk over. The air is cool on the crest of the field.

It's not large, the monument to Georgia troops who fought at Gettysburg—maybe fifteen feet from ground to top—but it's more stark and thick and imposing than I would have thought from Matt's newspapers, photos, or from the police file. It matches for a second the dark vertical presence on the edge of my vision. But it's not right. Too short, maybe, or too stout. And it's sunny now, which doesn't help it fit either.

The granite stone overlooks a declining meadow with a row of trees and that picket fence flanking it on either side. There are scattered saplings in the middle distance, and blue hills rolling away to what Dad says is the west. The stone is light gray except where it's in shadow. There it seems black. A pair of cannons flank either side, pointing east, marking the Confederate artillery line, guarding the dead and the bloodied fields they fought for.

I have no memory of seeing this place. I couldn't have. I was already dead when I was brought here. And once again I wonder, *Why?*

The monument itself consists of a thick flat rectangular base of stone, planted like a tabletop in the ground. Centered on top of this is a great square chunk of stone close to five feet wide and four feet tall. Each side of this has three shallow flutes cut into it. Above that is a smaller tier, a little less than a foot tall. Sitting atop that is a squared-off, eight- or nine-foot-tall column of gray stone that must weigh tons.

The whole thing breathes with a heavy sadness that crushes my chest.

"GEORGIA" is cut in block letters at the very top, and its state seal is below that. Etched into the stone around eye level are the weather-stained words:

GEORGIA CONFEDERATE
SOLDIERS
WE SLEEP HERE IN OBEDIENCE TO LAW;
WHEN DUTY CALLED, WE CAME,
WHEN COUNTRY CALLED, WE DIED.

I try to imagine someone placing my small body against the fluted cutouts on the front side of the base, the movements of arms and hands needed to set me there just so. I want to know more, I want to know all of it, but all I can really do is conjure the scene from Matt's lifeless photos, maps, reports, and diagrams.

Had the stone behind my back retained the cold of the

night before? It was November, so you'd think it would have, but the weather that year had been up and down, and the last days had been dry in the eastern part of the state, though not the west.

And since the police aren't certain of the hour I was put there, how long had it been before I was spotted, sitting calmly with my neck turned at an impossible angle?

Did birds spy me before anyone else? Did rabbits or deer wander up out of the woods and sniff at me? Early morning foxes running across the crisp November grass? Was the sky I might have seen if I were alive truly as blue as sapphire, as one newspaper said?

Matt snaps a picture on his phone. "Denis . . ."

I swing around to him—"*Yeah?*"—but he's talking to Dad.

". . . was on this side, wasn't he? The front side of the monument?"

Dad's big shoulders shrink forward, like he can't help it. Standing this way, he looks small. He's struggling to understand something about the monument other than what it means to everyone else—a memorial to soldiers who fought here over a hundred and fifty years ago.

"That's right, the front . . ." He lifts his eyes to the words. "Georgia . . . a place I hate more than anywhere in the world."

Then, with a single move, Dad takes Matt's hand in both of his. Matt wasn't expecting this. I imagine Dad needs to touch someone real, someone he is close to, to be right here when he digs up the past, his past in Georgia, the hated place, which is what he's about to do.

"So, growing up, you still want to know?"

Matt trembles, wondering how much he'll have to coax Dad. "Yes. Please."

"Then I'll tell you." This is said in a whisper, as Dad scans the inscription on the monument and reads the name at the top. "Most of it was regular. Boring. Sad. Most of it."

The words scare Matt. "You were in Georgia when you were small? But not long, right?"

"Till I was your age. Long enough." Dad draws in a slow breath, turns his head to see if Matt's listening, then breathes it out. "But it's really about my father. You need to know about my father. . . ."

21

VALDOSTA

With the sun hitting that block of stone, and moving under the sky and over the meadow and in their faces, Dad conjures his early life in ragged bits and pieces.

"It was raining, and there was this school bus," he begins, but he's already off-track. He stops, looks off, and blinks a couple of times. "Wait, sorry. Valdosta. That's where I lived. My father. You know, you and Denis weren't the f-first." He's stammering, trying to put together a story he never tells. "I mean, twins run in families, right? Well, my father and his brother, my uncle. They were twins too."

Matt is surprised, but knows there's more to come, so he reins it in. "You never talk about your uncle."

Dad snorts. "He died when he was a young man. I never

met him. I only know the stories. They were so different, so *unlike* each other, my grandmother told me. I was worried when you two were on the way . . . but you weren't anything like them, either of them. My uncle, Richard—Denis's middle name—he was his own person, she told me, calm, beautiful. He loved people, loved talking. My father just hated him when they were growing up. I guess he knew my uncle was gay, even when he was young, and he tortured him for it. This was before me, you understand. My father grew up angry, drank a lot. Was a drunk, really. I don't know what Vietnam did to him, but he was a hateful man, used to smack me around. This is your grandfather we're talking about."

"Dad, I'm so sorry."

"Yeah, well. He did a lot worse to my mother. It was almost lucky when she died. I was ten. In a car wash, would you believe it? When her car came out, she was slumped over the wheel."

"Dad!"

"She smoked a lot. After that, he really laid into me. Didn't hold back. I hated him. He was this wiry creep, skinny but strong. A sergeant when he was in the army. He couldn't keep a job. We fought. Once he slapped me to the floor because"—Dad laughs coldly here—"because I said that he was over thirty. It was an innocent remark, right? And I knew that only because my mother had said it, and I just repeated it. 'Dad's over thirty.' He slapped me. I was seven. That's how I grew up, being hit. Fighting. That was the real combat. That's what Georgia is for me."

Matt's face is streaming. Mine too. "Dad, what a junky way to live. But you got out. You've been a good dad to me. Us."

Dad screws up his face, remembering. "His mother, your great-grandmother, finally took me. I went to live with her in Pennsylvania."

Matt flicks his eyes at me. He remembers that GeeGee told me the same thing. "And you never went back? To Georgia, I mean. Except for the army?"

Dad glances at Matt, as if he's just realized he's not alone. "That's the point, Matt. I never wanted to go back, ever, after I moved in with my grandmother. Years later, your mother and I met, got married, moved to Buckwood. Then one day your mother calls me while I'm at work. She's out of her mind, screaming. She was pregnant with you, and she said my father was at our house. My father, drunk, and he came . . . at her . . ."

"Dad!"

"She said I needed to go after him. The last freaking thing I wanted to do was to go to Valdosta, but I had to. Your mother screamed at me that he attacked her, or almost. I had to go. When duty calls, right?"

Matt inhales a slow breath, trying to calm himself. "But did he? I mean, why—"

"So I tear down there. All day, into the night, I'm driving to Georgia. I look for him everywhere and find him the next morning, at a bar. This is eight o'clock. He's already skunked. I drag him out onto the sidewalk. It's pouring. I accuse him of assaulting Mommy."

Dad is back there in his mind now, he sees the street, he is screaming on the sidewalk.

"The rotten bum denies it. I'm sorry, Matt. I'm telling this like I remember it. He says he was just 'checking on her.' I punch his red drunk face, like I wanted to when I was little—"

He breaks off. It is minutes like this. No sound but the crows gathering in the trees behind us, calling raggedly.

Matt swallows. "Dad . . ."

"'The rain is pounding, and he's taunting me, 'You're like your uncle! Pansy!' And I really let him have it. He staggers back into the street. I'm ready to pound him again, when this bus, this morning school bus, comes around the corner. Maybe the bus is going too fast, but with the rain, it skids. I'm hit and thrown, but he steps right into it. The bus smacks him down and crushes his leg. Chops it right off . . ."

"My God, Dad!" Matt puts his arm around Dad's hunching shoulders, but our father is frozen in his story and doesn't feel it.

"I'm in the hospital in a coma. Eight weeks. When I wake up, my grandmother is there. My father died while I was in the coma."

Matt is shaking on his feet, picturing the vague features

of Dad's red-faced father, Mom back at the house, pregnant with us, the wet street, the bus, the leg.

"But if your father attacked Mom, you had to, right?"

"I don't know if he did. I don't know. The look in his eyes when I accused him was like I was wrong, I had it wrong. I hated that face, and I thought I knew he was lying, but it was too late. I kept hitting him. . . ."

"How bad . . . You weren't too badly hurt, really hurt, were you? You're strong now."

Dad blinks once, looks Matt in the face. "Banged up. Four broken ribs, fractured femur, pretty serious concussion. Subdural hematoma. I'm fine now." He blinks and seems to see the field for the first time in minutes. "After the hospital, I was . . . I was arrested. I went to jail because of the accident. They said I was partly responsible for it."

"Jail?" Matt is shocked at this, so am I. "Because your father died?"

Dad flicks his eyes away. "Three months, then probation. It would have been longer, but lawyers proved the bus driver had suffered blackouts before. I got out with time served. My grandmother changed toward me. I think she blamed me. She buried his ashes in her plot up here. All that was before you and Denis were born."

When he says my name, Dad shrinks inside himself, and the battlefield is so quiet between the words. I hear the crows again and the putter of a small plane and trucks shifting gears far away.

Soon it's just the two of them again, standing at the crest of the field, Matt's arm still on Dad's shoulders as if he's forgotten it's there. My chest is heaving from what Dad is telling, and what Matt is hearing, and I feel like I'm not wanted here. Like I'm eavesdropping.

"Just leave him alone," I whisper. "Let him forget."

But Matt keeps going. "The army was before that, right? Fort Benning?"

Dad stretches, and Matt finally draws his arm away. "Yeah. My squad had some really good guys from Fort Benning. I was lucky to get out of Afghanistan alive. Four guys in my squad were in a transport when it was blown to pieces, jerked into the air like a toy. Two were killed right there, two maimed. I was far enough away, but it could have been me. Bad, huh? One holy mess after another. It all leads back to Georgia. I hate that place."

"Dad, I'm so sorry. . . ."

Matt tries to reach out again, but Dad runs his hands over his chest, leans back on his feet, staggers, steadies himself by placing one hand flat on the stone, then traces his fingers into the words:

WHEN COUNTRY CALLED, WE DIED.

"I loved them, loved those guys, the way you do in battle. And I hated my father because of how he hurt people. My mother, my uncle when he was young. My father was that way his whole life. I'm happy he's gone."

He pounds the stone with his fist, bloodying his knuckles, until Matt hugs him tight to make him stop. "Dad, I'm so glad you're okay. I love you."

Dad rubs the blood from his fingers and breathes, as if for the first time in hours.

"It was you. Mom and you and Denis. Knowing you were at home waiting for me, that carried me through all of it."

22

THE GRAY STONE

Dad stands there, not feeling me near him, probably not even sensing Matt, not really. The dead stone block crushes him. It's the weight of how he grew up, of his father's death, of what happened to his comrades, of me. Unable to take in light or give it off, he slowly lowers himself to his knees, first one, then the other, like he's praying to the stone.

Matt can't see as I can how Dad is twisted and angry inside, but he knows. Sparks fly off our father like they flew from Matt that day at school, only a thousand times hotter. They're spitting in the air and on the ground like furious fire from an arc welder. They're the tangled confusion, anger, and shame burning his heart.

"Matt, tell Dad he didn't kill his father. It was his father's *own fault, or the bus driver's, or the rain's. Or God's. But not his. Tell him, Matt. He needs it."*

Matt is tongue-tied, but manages a few words. "Dad, none of it was your fault."

"Or Mom's, either, for forcing him to go there. It happened because of everything. It was all combined." I think of the innumerable threads. *"I don't know what it was. But say something!"*

"Dad, it wasn't you."

On that battlefield, it sounds weak, pathetic, untrue, and Dad stays kneeling. He doesn't move, as if he doesn't hear. The rain, late last night in Buckwood, must have fallen in Gettysburg a few hours later, and though it's sunny now, the ground is damp, and his knees soak into it. I sense him struggling for someone to tell him what on earth happened on that street in Valdosta and why I was killed and placed here and why, why, why, but there's no one to tell him anything.

He half turns his head to Matt. "In the car," he whispers.

"Please, Dad. Not yet?"

"No, in the car. In my bag. There's a folder. Bring it here. It's time you saw it."

Matt turns. He drags himself back to the car, tugs the door open, and unzips Dad's duffel, where he finds the file he's not supposed to know about. He brings it back, holds it out.

"Open it up. There are pictures. You can see them now."

At first I think Matt's hands shake only to pretend he

doesn't know what's in the folder, then I realize it's because he does know. He's studied those photos every night for two weeks. But now, at the very place where my body was found, the images cut him as he hasn't been cut before, and it hurts too much to keep the secret.

"I already saw the file, Dad," he chokes. "I found it in your room. I copied it. That's why I got in trouble at school. I'm sorry."

He didn't have to confess. He could easily have held it back, but he can't lie.

Still kneeling, not ready to rise, Dad looks up at him and nods a couple of times. "I guess I didn't hide it very well. Maybe I meant for you to find it. Don't tell Mom you've seen it. She's broken because of . . ." He sighs away the rest of what he might have said, but I hear it.

Poor Denis, my Denis.

He starts rocking.

"Matt, ask him something. He needs to get out of where he is. He's going to fall in. He's thinking about death too much. Death is my thing. It's not good for him."

Taking a step toward Dad, Matt puts his hand on his shoulder like a friend would do. I know he feels Dad's pain shoot into him. Matt is so old at this moment.

"You . . . you've come here a few times. . . ."

Dad wipes his face with both hands. This seems to take forever, then he stands up. "Every year, at least once. I never find anything. Never." He closes his eyes for a moment, then turns to the car. "Look, it was random. The killer left Denis here because he was afraid. Or he was low on gas. Or someone was coming. Or it was too dark to see. Or whatever. It's a dead end, Matt."

It's not a dead end, Matt thinks. It can't be. Denis was put here for a reason. He doesn't say this, but I hear him.

"Maybe," I say. "But this is enough for now. Let's get out of here. Just go home."

There's a lot of quiet after that, until a couple of cars drive up and people start milling around the spot, looking like they're waiting for us to move away.

One family has accents, so maybe they're from Georgia too, coming to pay their respects, although one blond-haired boy has all the junk of war—a toy musket with a rubber bayonet, a rebel cap, an ammo belt, a flintlock pistol stuffed into his waist. He runs away down the field.

"Was it here?" the wife asks her husband, and I hope to God they aren't here to visit the spot where my body was found.

But no. The husband sweeps his hands from the downward-sloping meadow to the trees. "This road marks the right flank of the Confederate line, the artillery position. My great-great whatever, the state senator, charged all the way to Little Round Top from here. Lost an eye and an arm in the Wheatfield. He was just a boy, then, in the 11th Georgia Infantry."

Dad smiles grimly at them and heads back to the car, not wanting any small talk. Matt follows for a step or two, then stops and whispers to me as softly as he can.

"Look how far away the Honda was. It's almost a mile from here."

"I think I know that."

"Yeah, but I didn't really see what a long way it was. He or they carried you all this way. Maybe there were two of them. That makes more sense. Two killers."

And a crack opens in my mind.

I hear the ragged voices of two men talking loudly at each other. Men with accents like the tourist husband from Georgia. I don't know where it was I heard them or when it was, but there are two voices. I press my memory, press it and squeeze it, and it hurts. But it comes.

A gray evening. Lights were glowing, I can't make out exactly where, and there was a sense that the weather was going to turn cold any minute. I was young and afraid of something. Maybe I was afraid of everything.

But I was alive and hearing voices, and one of them spits out that word.

I ain't hungry. Keep your muck.

The voice is rough and angry. *Ain't.* I dig deeper, scratch into the corners in my head, and suddenly, I hear more—this time from the second voice.

But here. It got all kind of cheese on it—

Idiot. It ain't even real cheese. You'll throw it up on your first ride.

These voices, two of them, come from far away, a noisy place, with jagged music, but over it all I hear that nauseating twang. *I ain't hungry. It ain't even real cheese. Your first ride.*

"Come on, Matt," Dad calls. "We should get home. Mommy doesn't like to be alone. Since Denis, she's worried about strangers."

I try to remember whoever carefully positioned my arms, my legs, my head. It doesn't fit with the harshness of *Keep your muck.* That comes from a different place. Here, I was set so gently, but I see no face in my mind, I hear no voice yet.

Only the word *cheese*, foul as it is in this place of grim death, sparks something real in me, and I understand we need to make another stop before going home to Mom.

We need to work back to the beginning, like GeeGee said.

To the place I first went missing. A place where they have rides. A place where they play music. Where they serve fake cheese.

Funland Amusement Park.

23

BY THE ROADSIDE

All told, we are on the battlefield only a little over an hour. While Dad drives on the highway back toward Buckwood, Matt reads the file and I prod from the back seat.

"The way to do this is to follow it back. GeeGee said so. We need to stop at the Big Dipper."

I ping and flick until Matt finally squirms away. "All right!" he snaps, then adds another "All right," like he's talking to Dad.

"Matt?"

"I'm just thinking. The last thing before Gettysburg, the last thing we know about—that *we* know about right now"— which is a dig at me, because he still thinks I *can* know more but I just *won't*—"is the roller coaster, right? The amusement park?"

Dad is eyeing two police cars down the road. Their lights are flashing. Several cars are pulled to the side. One officer trains a radar gun at passing cars, while the other leans in a minivan's window. Dad's driving is fine, but he cuts his speed.

"Right. Right. Beginning and end. Nothing in between."

I notice almost too late that one of the stopped vehicles is a gray pickup. We're by it too quickly to see if it has a dent in the driver's door like the one in Buckwood, but then, this is Pennsylvania, the land of dented pickups. I store it in the back of my mind.

"So, I don't know, maybe we should stop at Funland?" Matt says gently. "On the way home. It's not that late. To see if anything pops out at you. At us."

Dad's not fooled. "Okay, Matt, what's going on here? Gettysburg is one thing, but Funland?"

It sounds accusing, but the way he says it, it isn't. It's almost like Dad wants to be convinced that the two of them are on a kind of detective adventure, which I sense is something he's always wanted—to get into this with someone besides himself. He needs a companion in his pain. It isn't Mom anymore, not the way they are these days.

Matt picks up some of this. "I just think that it's five years, and maybe Mom, you know"—I realize this is the first time she's been mentioned in a while—"Mom is right. This should be it. The last time. Let's try to find something real about Denis, you and me, but if we don't, that's it. We love Denis, but one more stop, then it's over, and we move on."

I suddenly don't like those last three words.

"We can help each other move on," Matt adds.

I don't like those even more.

I came here to tell Matt to back off. Now it strikes me that if he *does* back off, if they all *move on*, the threads between us will fray and fray and soon I won't be anywhere. GeeGee was so gray and little when I left. How long before that happens to me?

Dad is quiet, gradually picking up speed after the police cars by the roadside. He ponders what Matt's saying, works it over, imagines if he even *can* give up searching for the answer to my death. Then he surprises me. "Well, I'll have to tell your mother we'll be home really late. But yeah, let's make this the final tour."

Matt nods. "Cool, Dad. Thanks."

Fine. I get it. It's the way it should be. After this little jaunt, no more me. I slink into the seat and pout.

But I perk up when after a few miles Dad says, "One thing you won't find in the file is anything about this." He taps the chain around Matt's neck.

"Your dog tag?"

"You probably don't even remember, you've been wearing it so long. When you were little, three or something, you and Denis found these, you little snoopers. My tags from the army. I had to give you each one."

Matt tugs the tag out and reads it. "Yeah. I remember. How come there are two?"

"One's collected for notification—if you die—and the other stays with the body. If you live, you get to keep both of them. Denis was missing his when they found him."

"Missing? Really? Dad, that's important."

"I didn't tell the police it was missing."

"Why not?"

Dad has gradually reduced his speed, and cars are passing quickly and noisily on the left. "I . . . I actually don't know. Maybe because it was Georgia, right? The army. My father? I don't know. Mommy didn't notice it was missing. I didn't see the point. It was probably just lost."

Matt is quiet for a mile or so. "I guess I get that. Yeah."

"We'll be at Funland in about two hours."

"Cool. Thanks again, Dad."

Matt turns to me by pretending he's shifting in his seat. *"Dab's father and ankle are dead,"* he says from inside his head. *"His Georgia war bubbies were good guys. Who arse is leff? Who could it pee?"*

"Yeah, you gotta work on your mind-talking. But I don't know. It's not like I can time travel back to a place where something happened. I can only see what people let me see inside them. There might be more, but Dad's way too dark about that stuff."

"*Maybe his fazzer knows,*" Matt says. "*You cam find him in Plot Haven. He's gotta be up there, because Dad sure dismembers him. You can find him if you want to.*"

And suddenly the idea of talking to that angry man scares me, though I know he probably wouldn't be very angry anymore. You lose that, more or less, when you croak.

"*Yeah,*" I say. "*Maybe.*"

The truth is, I feel dirty trying to assemble this ugly past, like sewing people together after they've been blown to pieces. I know I need to go back to my real home, but I don't want to.

Not yet.

24

THE BIG DIPPER

It's midafternoon and cloudy by the time we drive into Funland, which is open for another few hours. All the way up the road, we see the vast bone-white skeleton of the Big Dipper rolling and arching over the trees and other rides.

Dad parks in the lot but doesn't get out. We sit and look. Something about the time of day tingles in my mind. The sun is still up, but I'm pretty sure it wasn't five years ago.

"Matt. It was dark when we came here before, wasn't it? That time?"

He turns to me in the dying light. "How did you nose that?"

"I'm not sure. Strings of lights looping on things?"

He goes for it. "Dad, we stayed late that day, didn't we?"

Dad surfaces from wherever he is, shifts in his seat, and thinks for a bit. "It was late, and the park closed earlier than usual. The fire. That was part of the problem. Crowds rushing as we searched for him."

Matt nods slowly, remembering.

We finally exit the car. The lot is a third full. Music and light draw us to the entrance gate.

Other structures are visible now, medieval facades and haunted houses and garish carousels of different sizes. A couple of wild "Heated Water Rides!" with winding yellow chutes and great statues of jungle animals. Rockets and whirling swings and pendulum rides and giant slides.

And a drop tower rising up into the sky like a steel column, which reminds me instantly of that thing on the edge of my left eye.

"Matt, did we go on the tower?"

He repeats the question, but Dad says we never did, and I realize the tower was not quite right after all, because the glittery lights strung up on it are too playful. The thing in my eye is menacing and bleak.

From the dark, the darker darkness rises.

Over the intense whine of machines and shrieking music and screaming voices, the weirdly sinister Big Dipper looms. It is like a thing from another world.

"The Dipper is where we should start," Dad says. "Maybe we'll get an idea up there."

But as Dad pays and the two of them pass into the park, I get the sense he's shifting away from detective. Not that he wants to, but he's loved roller coasters all his life—maybe he got that love from his grandfather, GeeGee's husband, who built coasters—and no matter how much this ride has to do with me, his heart lifts a little at the sight of it. But that's okay. Dad needs to think about something besides me, even if everything here is about me.

"These blue safety lights are new," he says, motioning to wooden posts standing here and there with blue lights on them. "You see them at colleges. If you're in trouble or think you are, you run to one, press a button, and security comes. They installed them after Denis."

So.

I made a difference.

We walk to the Dipper and I feel breathless, as if a dark thing is suddenly thrown over me, like I've dropped into a sinkhole. Or, not a hole, but a tight space, shut away from the world.

Is this a random feeling or a memory?

I stop short on the green-painted path, people swirling happily past me. What in the world happened those three days between when I went missing and when I was discovered? Where are the scattered yellow leaves? The glint of something silver? The ash drifting across my eyes?

I stare at my feet, close my eyes, and fall inside myself. I hear a raucous jumble of noises, something whines, and there is grinding, the slide of feet in dirt or gravel, swearing, a muffled drone, a bright red fever behind my eyes.

Suddenly, it's as if my mind took a breath after holding it forever, and I'm flooded with the air and noise and the smell of evening and food, and the clattering and music of five years ago.

25

WOODEN BONES

We had arrived late at the park that day. Why?

Because because because.

We weren't going to go anywhere at all the Sunday before Thanksgiving. I remember Dad had been away for a few days and the yard was cluttered with leaves. After church he and Matt and I spent the morning raking them. Only after bagging them to eventually take to the dump, and Dad was reading the paper on the patio, did someone get the amazing idea to go to Funland. Who was it, after all? Me? Did I choose the place of my own kidnapping?

Dad jumped at the idea. "Oh man, coasters! The Big Dipper is completely the best!"

By then, though, Mom was at the grocery store, starting

her holiday food shopping. Even when we finally got on the road, Dad had to stop at the bank for cash. Then for gas. Then Matt had to pee, then Dad said he had to also, which caused Mom to swat him, but we stopped anyway.

It was nearly four in the afternoon when we got to the park and everyone was superhungry, but there it was, the bony wooden track of the Dipper rising above everything else, and Matt and I freaked at the old-time beauty of it.

Funland's major attraction, the Big Dipper, was another kind of historical monument from ages ago. They let you see it from all angles, but you had to wade through everything else and use all your tickets before you got to it, so you had to buy more to get on the big ride.

As we trotted after Dad to the coaster that afternoon, I remember the moment we heard a sudden squeal of funny horns, and Matt cried out, "I want to drive the clown cars!"

What if we had? What would be different now?

"After the coaster," Dad insisted. "You have to ride it first. Then we'll do everything else. That's the smart way. Seriously, Matt. You'll love it."

Mom laughed. "As if we have a choice!"

"What you don't understand," Dad said, "is that the Big Dipper was the tallest wooden roller coaster in the country when it was built in 1926. A hundred and three feet at its height." He sounded like a tour guide, talking at us over his shoulder as he wove through bunches of families. "It has two long dips on the course, both into natural ravines. One is forty-eight feet from the crest to the bottom. The other is seventy-two feet. Seventy-two! That's more than twice as tall as our house."

Seven-year-old Matt was impressed. "Whoa."

"You're darn right, whoa. On a clear day you can see miles of countryside from the top. Forests, hills, the center of some town; Hunker, maybe. A train to the north. My grandfather—your great-grandfather—did repair work on the Big Dipper over the years. He helped design a mine close to where I grew up. There's a lot of Egan sweat in this part of the state. I just love how far our family goes back in Pennsylvania." He smiled at Mom, then at the two of us. "I look at you boys, and think how far you'll go on from here."

"Kind of ick, Dad," said Matt.

Dad was almost manic, really bouncing around like I used to in school. Maybe I inherited that habit from him, but he was especially bouncy that day, going from one thing to another, a bit over the top. Maybe it was the business trip he'd just come back from. Maybe five days away had made him extra happy to be with us again.

"Dad," I said, "Dad, why do they call it the Big Dipper?"

I knew the answer, we all did. It was a thing we used to ask and Dad would always answer, as he did again that day:

"Because it dips. Big!"

Mom rolled her eyes. "So show us this famous coaster, already."

"That's the thing. It isn't famous at all!" he said, laughing in a way that startles my ear now that I'm remembering it. It was the full, deep laugh of a man who, despite his past, loved that he had a happy wife and two bright, funny twin boys. I feel my heart ache now as I remember this.

"It isn't famous," he repeated, "but it should be. It's the least attended old coaster in the state, but one of the absolute best. And not just because my grandfather worked on it. Though he did work on it. By the way, did I ever tell you who worked on it?"

"Who?" I asked.

"My grandfather."

"Did he?" said Matt.

"He did. My grandfather worked on it. Forward, march!"

Second by second the day comes back. I see Dad hustling ahead while keeping us in view. I remember the moment Mom suddenly stopped.

"Food. Food first, Gary, oh, please!"

Dad groaned. "Who's hungry? You're not hungry, are you?"

"Corn dogs!" I said.

Dad shakes his head. "You're taking a big risk, eating before the coaster. You can drink something. I might have a beer, but how can you be hungry? I'm not hungry!"

I guess it's at this moment, remembering what Dad had said five years ago at the park, knowing it's so like what someone who might have hurt me said, that I really remember things. The whole day begins to roar back over me.

I ain't hungry. Keep your muck.

That's the moment I begin to die.

26

A BOY THING

So Matt and I stuffed ourselves on corn dogs, Mom had a cheeseburger, and Dad ordered a beer, which quickly turned into two beers that he finished while we ate.

"That's it," he said, tossing his second cup into the recycling bin. "Dipper time!"

He nearly pushed people over to get to it, apologizing and laughing. We waited, not so patiently, and when the cars came around and emptied, he darted through the gate, found a seat, plunked down, and seemed to forget about us. He was acting like a kid; it was almost fun to watch. I wonder now how many beers he'd actually had.

Mom wasn't interested in going on. "It's a boy thing," she said with a laugh. "No, it's not. I just don't want to. Besides,

I'm still finishing my burger."

Matt and I went on the coaster twice with Dad, but even we didn't want to get dipped into a bottomless ravine three times. So we left him laughing as he made his way to the front for a third ride.

The guy running the Dipper said it was fine, since Dad gave him tickets for six rides. The coaster wasn't full—it was November—and the late-season rules were loose.

We stayed on the platform to wait for Dad. We were there only a few minutes before Matt turned green and clutched his stomach. "It was that third corn dog!" I razzed him while he and Mom scurried to the restrooms at the end of the boardwalk along the tracks. I said I'd wait for Dad.

The line thickened while I waited. There was a crowd now. The coaster rolled in. I called to Dad, but he was staying on. I didn't want to stand alone on the platform, so just before the coaster started off, I gave the guy my last ticket and jumped into the end car.

Does this mean anything, my impulsive move to hop on the coaster without Dad seeing me do it? Did Dad's decision to go for one more ride after he saw me alone change things? Was Matt's third corn dog the real problem? Puzzling it over now, I'm not sure of anything.

The coaster rose and dived and swung and dipped, and now my supper started to slosh around. As amazing as my great-grandfather's ride was, I had really had enough.

I stumbled out of the car only to find that Dad stayed on for a fifth ride. I didn't see Matt or Mom on the platform. Outside the ladies' room, I asked a woman to tell my mom I was waiting, but she said the stalls were empty. I needed to go now, so I went in. Matt wasn't there either. When I came out minutes later, the ride had either not returned or had started again.

I waited. No Dad.

"Your father left," the guy running the coaster finally said. "Before."

My chest shuddered. I was in a big place without my parents.

"He left?"

"He did," said a lady with two girls. "He was looking for you."

"Your brother left with your mother," the guy said. "You're identical."

"Do you need help?" the lady said. She started to get out of line.

"No thanks," I said, trying to be brave. "They must be near here."

"Go to a policeman," said one of her daughters, the younger one.

"I will. Thanks."

I slipped through the gate and left the coaster boardwalk, my head swiveling every which way to catch sight of them. They couldn't have gone far. I hurried down the stairs through a gate and stepped onto the dusty pavement, looking for Dad's big shoulders or Mom's wavy brown hair, but not seeing either.

My heart beat out a crazy rhythm, thumping, stuttering. Dad might have been the nearest to where I was, but he was also a runner, so he might be the farthest. Matt had to be with Mom, but who knew where by now.

I remember all this, but also that Russell and GeeGee told me it's dangerous to remember too much. Memory runs through you, changes you, thickens you. The razor will damage you more the more weight you put on and rip, rip, rip, you fly apart. The guy with pink hair said that. But dangerous or not, I have to follow what I remember—for Matt, for Mom and Dad.

In my memory I hear a voice.

"Sweetie. Hey, sweetie!"

A woman behind the counter of a small booth called to me. She was short and round, had several chins beneath the smilingest face. Stuffed toys were pinned up on the inside walls of her booth. The booth was called Pitch-em Fast! The exclamation point was part of the name. She was wagging one bare arm at me, while her other hand held a giant pink sipper cup. "Over here. You look lost. You lost? Where your people? Thirsty?" She offered me her pink cup, still waving me over. There was no one at her booth, or she probably wouldn't have noticed me.

"I can't find my parents and my brother—"

She cackled. "Happens all the time. Your name? Don't you worry."

"Egan," I said.

"What were your parents thinking? Egan what?"

"No. Denis Egan. My mom is tall with wavy brown hair—"

"Ha! Ain't we all, honey. Hold up." She switched on a walkie-talkie she pulled from beneath the counter. "Care for a throw?" She patted a set of three worn tennis balls. Plastic milk bottles were stacked along a shelf at the back of the booth. "Knock 'em down and get a stuff toy."

I scanned the moving crowds, feeling so alone, abandoned, even, knowing it was a thousand times different from hiding in the small woods behind our house. "No thanks—"

"Hold up," she repeated, speaking into her talkie. "Benjy? Lost boy, aisle seventeen, booth nine." She pulled the talkie away from her face. "How old you, son? What's your mom's name?"

You understand, I am remembering all this as if I'm wearing smeared-up glasses, while Matt and Dad walk alone through the aisles, looking for clues that can't possibly be here anymore.

As the booth lady asked me that—"What's your mom's name?"—I caught sight of two men standing a few booths down the aisle of games. They looked alike in the face, both unshaven, same nose, Pirates baseball caps, but one was thin as a stick, and the other had a belly like a sandbag hanging over his belt.

"Bonnie," I told the woman. "Bonnie Egan."

"Sounds like a movie star name. Pretty, huh?"

"I guess . . ."

"Yeah, you guess. Wavy brown hair and all."

There was no one playing the booths between me and the two men. I felt so small. This was the skeevy part of the amusement park, where you used up tickets fast on dumb games rigged against you.

Then, out of the corner of my eye, I watched the skinny guy take a grease-stained container, cup it under his chin, and lick the inside.

Cheese.

Sandbag Stomach tossed darts at balloons tacked up against the back of the booth. That game was called Pop-Pop-Pop!

Also with an exclamation mark.

"Here you go," the skinny guy said, holding out the container.

Sandbag snorted. "I ain't hungry. Keep your muck."

"But here. It got all kind of cheese on it—"

"Idiot. It ain't even real cheese. You'll throw it up on your first ride."

Stick laughed, continued licking out the container, then saw me watching him. But his look was off-center, as if one eye didn't work right.

"They'll be here pronto, security," the lady said. "You stay close now."

"Thank you."

Both guys were staring at me.

"Hey, come on over!" the lady called to them. "Win a stuffed toy."

They sauntered toward us, laughing to each other like they'd just pulled something off. One-Eye tilted his face so he could keep his good eye on me. I stepped back to the far end of the counter, but I got a whiff of them. The stink of cigarettes and sweat and unclean underwear. They laughed nastily while the lady took their tickets and tucked them under the counter.

Not liking the way they looked at me, I rounded the corner, then slid around the side of the booth and trotted down the aisle behind, until I came to the end of the row. My heart was beating insanely. Five different songs blared from five different speakers.

I slowed down to reset myself and look for Matt and Mom and Dad.

Then I spied Sandbag, planted at the end of the aisle ahead of me, his hands on his hips. I stole a look behind. One-Eye loped slowly toward me, finally tossing his nacho container to the ground. They were boxing me in. Reggae music thumped. I slipped into the sliver of space between two booths and came out at Pop-Pop-Pop! My hands clenched and unclenched. I had to get out of there.

"Mom!" I yelled as loudly as I could, then realized it wasn't specific enough. "Matt!" My voice was tiny and went nowhere. "Matt Egan!"

"S'cuse me hey boy you lost?" One-Eye's whiny voice came out of his nose. I didn't want to turn and look at him, but it's what you do.

I blurted out, "I don't know you. You're thinking of somebody else."

"Thass okay. We'll help you."

I shot through to the next aisle and looked for a police officer or a man in a suit, but all I saw were families and barkers and crowds of high schoolers who didn't care about a lost kid who anyway reminded them of the little brother they were glad to be rid of for a night.

I kept moving. An older man in a rumpled blue jacket was talking to a teenager whose hands held the controls of the merry-go-round. The kid had spiked hair, and he nodded as if the old guy was his boss. I looked behind me. The two men had joined up again. When I turned back, the man in the jacket was through a gate to another ride, then another. I ran after, but my legs were stupid wooden sticks. I was unable to catch up.

Then I saw Mom.

"Mom!" I yelled. "Mommy!"

She had her arm around Matt. His head was down. Was he still sick from corn dogs? Why weren't they looking for me? I slowed, shouted for Dad. People turned their heads. Other dads, not mine. My heart nearly burst open. I yelled. "Mom! Mom!" But she and Matt pushed out the entrance gate and into the parking lot. Did they think I was outside? Where was Dad?

"Mom!" I shouted. She kept hurrying. Matt was pulled deep into her side, half doubled over, like he was ready to throw up. I must have been farther away than I thought because I couldn't seem to catch them, either. Then with one hand Mom tugged at her bag, pulled out her keys, and beeped open a blue car.

Blue car?

Our car was light brown.

"Matt!" I called. He didn't turn around. "Matt!"

Mom hurried around to help Matt into the passenger seat. It wasn't Matt. The woman I thought was Mom wasn't Mom. Brown hair, same height, not Mom. She started the car. They pulled out and drove away.

I felt something break inside me. My chest flooded with ice water. I was outside the park now. I'd done everything right. Found a person in charge. Searched for a police officer. I found my mother and ran to her, but she wasn't my mother.

Looking around, I couldn't see the two creeps anywhere in the parking lot. I knew I should get back inside where everyone was. I waited in line at the entrance to talk to the woman there. She had gray hair, glasses, several rings on her fingers. Then she said, "I haven't seen your brother. Denis, his name was?"

"What? No, *I'm* Denis. That's me. Was my brother looking for me?"

"You're identical—"

"I know that! Where is he?" I craned my neck to see over the fence.

"He was crying. His mother was too. Your mother. Look, I'll make an announcement," she said. She lifted up the phone. At that moment, just that moment, there was a shout from inside the park. Someone came running. The ticket woman held the phone from her face.

"The haunted house is down!" an older boy said in a panic. He was the same one from the merry-go-round. Spiked hair. It's like a dream now. "Some guy had a fight with Benjy. The police are on their way. Plus, there was a fire behind the coaster. They're closing the park."

Announcements had already begun to screech over the address system.

"My parents must be going crazy," I said. "I need to get back inside!"

The woman looked me over with a strange expression on

her face, as if she'd suddenly forgotten who I was. She was old, but not that old. "Lady!" I said. I felt invisible, unable to get them to hear me. Maybe I wasn't talking correctly. Maybe I was so afraid I was just crying.

The next thing I knew, the woman was shouting at the people in the line behind me, still holding the phone away from her face, almost unaware she was holding it. She told me to wait outside the gate "while I keep an eye on you." The old coaster wove around so many other rides, she explained, that "even a small fire means the whole park's gotta shut down because security's needed all over the place."

Because because because.

Then she gave me a flat smile and put the receiver down on the base and shut the ticket window. It was stupid, but that's what she did.

I backed up with the others, some of whom were grumbling, while some were videoing the feathers of smoke rising from the park.

I moved to get clear of the crowds pouring from the gate, when an arm clamped across my chest from behind. I was pulled back so fast I couldn't make a sound before a big hand cupped over my mouth.

"Sonny," a voice rasped. "Good thing we finally found you!"

"I don't know you!" I tried to shout, but it came out like a squeak.

Cars were moving, people were rushing out the exits, and no one noticed the two men drag me away in a chokehold. I was terrified. Maybe I peed myself, I didn't know. I smelled popcorn and cigarettes and maybe myself.

I tried to shout, to bite the hand over my mouth. Before I could wiggle free, a fist slammed my temple, and the inside of my eyes went black.

27

MOTORING AWAY

I woke up in the dark and the dark was moving.

My blood had turned to ice. I felt naked, empty, lost, I don't know what.

Thick strips of tape had been stretched over my eyes and wound around my head to the tip of my nose and over my mouth. My heart pounded fast and hard.

I stretched, tried to. My arms were tied behind my back, and my hands were taped together. I smelled the odor of exhaust. I was in the trunk of a car. It was seeping exhaust too much to be new, and the walls were close to me. An older compact car.

I didn't want to breathe through my nose, but my mouth

was sealed shut, so I had to. I kicked once, only to find that a rope was tied between my ankles and my neck.

We bounced hard. My shoulder struck the roof of the trunk. Yes, a small car. The trunk roof was jagged, too. My shoulder stung. Tetanus, I thought. That's the shot you need when you cut yourself on something rusty. The car slowed, sped up, slowed again. I listened for any kind of clue to where they were taking me. I had no sight, not much touch, but I could breathe and hear.

"Denis."

I'm startled out of that frightening darkness. I turn my face from Matt and try to regain the trunk, but the memory fades there, with the car rolling and rolling. My chest aches now, like it did then. Maybe I'd gone unconscious anyway. Anyway, I can't remember more. It's gone.

"Denis," he insists. "Dad is . . ."

I come out of myself to see Dad leaning hard on the fence around a ride, his hands clutching the top rail like he wants to rip it off. When he straightens, it's clear he's drained to the core.

"*They took me away in a car,*" I say in Matt's head.

"The Honda?" he whispers.

"*My guess. An older one.*" I tell him about the two disgusting men, the accents they have, the others who tried to help, the ones who didn't, the parking lot, the fire, all of it, up until the moment I blacked out in the trunk. Matt listens, mouth open, searching the light to pin me down.

Dad approaches Matt slowly, his shoulders bowed with the weight of my body. "Did anything come back to you?" His voice is hoarse and he looks ready to drop.

I wonder how Matt will tell him about the two men. Will he blurt out my memories of that night, which he couldn't possibly know? Or will he be smart in a way I can't begin to imagine?

As they walk to the entrance, he's smart about it.

"Dad, I'm thinking back, and you know how Denis sort of disappeared while I was in the bathroom throwing up and you were on the coaster?"

Dad nods, slips his hand into his pocket, and jingles his keys with his fingers. "I should never have gone on the stupid coaster. Not again and again and again like an idiot."

"Mom and I weren't there either."

"You were sick. What was my excuse? Beer? I was his father."

Matt doesn't look at him. How do you respond to a parent who digs at himself this way? Dads are supposed to be strong, always. Matt presses on.

"Well, I think if everyone was leaving the park, because of the fire, maybe Denis was caught up in that. So he was probably in the parking lot too. Mom and I didn't see him. When we asked at the entrance booth, the lady hadn't seen him either, but later she said she did."

We slip through the exit turnstiles and are in the lot as the night crowd thins out.

"She also said she remembers letting him back into the park," Dad says.

"She was wrong. I mean, what if she was confused? There was a fire and everything. And she was old. She didn't remember right."

"She wasn't that old."

Of course, my thoughts go right to GeeGee, the last time I saw her, her forgetfulness. The ticket lady wasn't as old as her, but she wasn't young.

"Anyway, what does all that tell you?" Dad asks.

"Make sure you don't say trunk—"

"What if Denis was already in somebody's trunk?"

Dad stops. "Trunk? Matt, we can't know that. There's no proof of that."

"But maybe the kidnappers took Denis right after the fire started and disappeared while we were still searching for him inside. People were rushing around, weren't they?"

Dad frowns and tugs out his keys. "Possibly, yeah. I don't know. I need to think about it. I'll reread the file." He looks around, sighs all the air from his lungs. "I'm beat. You must be tired too. We've done a lot of driving today. We should leave now, go home. I'll call Mom."

Matt stops dead. "I also remember a couple of sketchy guys lurking around the park that day. Creepy men. They talked with accents. Southern, sort of. Being here made me remember."

"Really? Why the heck didn't you ..." Dad pauses, thinks. "No, that's good, Matt. Memories can sneak up on you, can't they? Let's try to put this together while we drive, okay?"

When he beeps the car open I have a sudden idea.

"I'm getting in the trunk."

"What?"

Dad turns. "Matt?"

"Uh, nothing. Just ... arguing with myself."

"I need to be in the trunk. To see what memories come sneaking up, right?"

Before Matt can say anything, I ooze into the trunk, squirrel myself up, contorting myself as if I were tied, and jam my eyes shut. It works. As the car wheels out of the lot, I fall backward, sinking and sinking into the dark past.

28

THEM KIDNAPPERS

One-Eye and Sandbag kept arguing viciously in the front seat, using foul words you wouldn't believe. They always seemed ready to pound each other. I shifted as far forward as I could without choking myself, trying to hear anything important. Feeling the miles pass, I also began to wonder how long I'd been out cold, when it dawned on me that after wetting myself in the parking lot, I hadn't gone again and didn't have to, which meant it wasn't too long after I was taken. It felt good to know that. Taking stock of myself, I realized the side of my head hurt where I was hit, and both my arms.

And there was the tooth.

They'd cracked my lower left canine, either with a head

punch or when they dropped me in the trunk. The tooth was loose and chipped. My lip was cracked and swollen. I swallowed blood. I worked the jagged edge with my tongue, thinking the pain would keep me awake. I felt like throwing up the acid in my stomach, but I held back, breathed slowly, and tried to calm myself.

One thing helped more than anything: that even though every inch of my body, inside and out, ached like nothing ever had, I had taken it, I *was* taking it, and I was still alive and thinking.

Suddenly, the car bounced once, hard, then again. It jerked to a stop.

By the way the weight shifted, I figured it was One-Eye who got out. I then heard knocking next to my ear, followed by a roar of liquid and the smell of gasoline. If they filled up the tank, it might mean they were going to drive a long time. But no. The roar lasted far less than a minute, and at the end of it there was the pump, stop, pump, stop that I'd seen Dad do to get an exact dollar amount of gas.

Then One-Eye swore. "I went over a bit. Gimme a quarter."

They were paying cash, and not a lot of it.

I kicked to make a sound while we were at the station, but the yank on my neck made me gag. One-Eye banged the trunk lid to stop me. A couple of minutes later, he was back in the car.

They tore away and began speeding up, which scared me. If we got on a highway, I'd totally lose track of where we might be, but it never got very fast, and soon the car was clanking over what sounded like metal plates.

A bridge! GeeGee said my great-grandfather built bridges, and I think now how strange it would be if I rode over one of his. From his coaster to his bridge.

Did I think about GeeGee at that moment, as I do now?

No. I didn't know her back then.

The car wasn't long on the bridge—so the river or creek underneath was narrow—before we hit rough pavement again. There was a short straight with a little S in it, then two rights, left, right, left, and slowing way down, as we bumped on crunchy stones, where the car finally wobbled to a stop. It idled in place, fuming exhaust into the back. The men began yelling again. Sandbag must have lashed out because I felt a shift of weight, and One-Eye went quiet.

Vehicles backed up around us, drove off, drove in. A truck stop? No, they weren't heavy engines. Cars. I was playing detective again, except not playing. Sandbag turned off the motor and hoisted his gut out. One-Eye came around to the back and sat on the trunk. Cigarette smoke. A minute or two passed before Sandbag returned, then One-Eye got back in, and the doors squealed shut. The car started up.

"Which one?" One-Eye asked, speaking from his nose.

"Seven. Last one on the left," Sandbag growled like an

animal. "I axed him for the end one."

"You *axed* him for it?"

"Shut up!"

The car rumbled slowly over more bumps, but only for a half minute before it stopped again. The engine sputtered a little, then shut off. Smoke in the trunk. I held my breath as long as I could, then sniffed shallowly. The car doors swung open.

The men stood by the trunk. Sandbag slammed his fist on it and laughed. "Soon, honeybunch!" he said to me. This scared my blood cold. I called out in my head, *"Daddy! Daddy!"* He would find me wherever I was. Somehow he would follow me and rescue me. He would get in the car and drive, right, left, over a bridge, all the time hunched over the wheel and on fire, like he went after his father.

He would.

They slid bags out of the back seat. Footsteps ground into loose stone. There was a wide strip of gravel beside the car, I heard shoes slide and crackle through it. A jingle of keys. Were we at a motel? I remember now how I really hoped they thought I was someone else, and once they realized I wasn't who they wanted, they'd let me go. Why would they want *me* anyway?

"Daddy, find me!"

Their feet left the gravel for a wooden step, and I heard the spring of a screen door. Maybe not a motel. They don't have gravel-covered lots or steps to rooms or screen doors. Number seven. Last one on the left.

A cabin?

In between noises I heard birds. Three or four crows cawing overhead, flying toward the car. They must have lighted on something because they stayed for a bit, making a racket before they flew off. Then it was quiet.

It had to be early evening by then, or later. It was November and it was getting dark when the amusement park closed down an hour or more ago. But there were people walking here, and cars driving in and out, so it wasn't crazy late. Then I had a weird thought. Was it bedtime yet? I thought of Matt still being up, wondering what had happened to me. He couldn't sleep. How could he sleep? But never mind that. It was far more important to remember what I heard and felt every second I was awake, which sure helps me now that I try to reconstruct that day.

Putting it together, there was a short steel bridge, followed by zigzagging slow roads, then cabins—maybe cabins—ten or so minutes from a gas station, all of which were not more than an hour from Funland.

Dad is busy driving as I ooze into the back seat and touch Matt creepily on the neck, which I do because I can. He nearly shrieks, then makes it seem like he just woke up.

"Oh, sorry, Dad."

"No, that's fine. I need to stop for some gas about soon."

After a few miles they pull into a rest area, where Dad slides his card into the slot, and pumps.

"So?" Matt shifts his hair out of his eyes, finding me in a sliver of streetlight. "What did you come up with?"

"They drove, but not long. Maybe no more than twenty or thirty miles, if that. As far as I remember they never got on a highway. There was a gas station. They paid cash. Then they crossed a short bridge, and soon went to some kind of place where they have cabins or cottages. Sandbag drove, probably because One-Eye couldn't drive without both eyes. They took me there and maybe spent the night. It was late, the same night, Sunday, and it was getting quiet."

Matt shakes his head over and over. "You were seven. You must have been scared out of your mind. How could you remember a single thing?"

"I don't know. I thought I needed to, so you could find me."

He jams his eyes closed. "Denis, I'm so sorry."

"It's over now."

But as I say that, I know how wrong I am. I'm remembering what led up to my death five years ago, and these memories are going to hurt me. I feel the razor blade angrily waiting to slice my face, and it scares me cold.

"Is there anything else? Like did they kidnap you for ransom?" His voice cracks. "Then just decide to . . . murder you?"

And for the first time, that word—*murder*—sounds oddly wrong in my mind, though I don't know why it should. Am I trying to spare myself? The whole world calls my death a murder, so shouldn't I call it that too?

"I guess," I tell him. "But there's still the shadow. That wasn't in the trunk. And if the flakes I see *are* snow, and it first snowed Tuesday, I'm out of the car by then. I still had my tooth, too."

"That's good, real good."

"Let's find those cabins," I say, then change registers. *"Shh. Here's Dad."*

He arrives with snacks and says, "I called Mommy and told her we'd be back later."

"How did she seem? Mad?"

"Not too." Dad smirks, like he and Matt are in this together, which I guess they are. "If we come home in the next couple of hours."

Matt nods, wondering how to get him to look for cabins. What is he going to say? How would Matt know about cabins? Then hits on this: "Maybe we could take back roads, though, to make it last a little longer?"

Dad frowns, and I wonder for a moment if I should help out and simply appear to him and prove we're on the right track. I get that it won't be good for me, but as the tension twists tighter and tighter inside him, I realize that no matter how I might try, Dad may not even see me.

"Sure," he says finally. "Matt and Dad. The last tour."

He starts the car, and we drive off into the falling darkness.

29

IN THE BOONDOCKS

While Dad motors meanderingly north toward Buckwood, Matt searches his phone for cottages and maps them, then goes to satellite imagery to find a nearby bridge, all without letting on what he's doing.

He finds something.

"*There are four motor corns within two hours of Fanland,*" Matt says in my head.

"I love motor corns, but you probably mean motor courts?"

"*Sorry. Trying to get the hand off this thong. Hang. Hang of this thong. Thing!*"

"*Four motor courts are too many. Dad won't go to all of them.*"

"Well, then it's hopeless," he blurts aloud.

Dad has been silent since the gas station. "What is?"

Matt thinks on his feet. "If they—or he or whoever—kidnap Denis in a car, they could take him anywhere. But maybe it's too late at night to send any kind of ransom demand, even if they know where to send it. What if they stayed somewhere?"

"Somewhere. Anywhere. The police set roadblocks and checkpoints, ran credit cards. Some people paid admission with cash. They couldn't get everyone's identity or search every home."

"But maybe the kidnappers didn't go home," Matt says. "Maybe they don't want to be tracked. Besides, they'd already gone. Probably. But where did they stay? If it *was* those creepy guys I think I saw, it wouldn't be anywhere too nice."

I have to hand it to the kid. Little by little he's circling the idea of cabins in the boondocks.

Dad shakes his head. "Except that trail goes cold, too. The cops never found a direction. Denis was just . . . gone. . . . He vanished until the battlefield three days later. Matt, I don't know if we're getting anywhere. We're not far from Buckwood. Call Mom and tell her we're on our way. It'll be better if she hears your voice."

"I will," Matt says, giving me a side glance. "In a bit."

He needs more. While he searches his maps for some

kind of clue, I slip through the back seat into the trunk again. Being shut in the suffocating space ripples through me, and I'm back outside cabin seven, at the end on the left.

I still couldn't shift my body or make much noise. All my energy went into breathing. An hour passed, more. My legs and arms went cold, then numb. No bird calls anymore. It had to have been past midnight at this point. Four cars rolled in over the gravel, two others started up and left, their motors sputtering, but none of them were close enough to hear any sound I might make. Later, a couple of teenagers shouted, and there came a clatter of pots and pans. I'm more convinced than ever that I was taken to a cottage complex far out in the country.

Sometime after that, I heard clacking in the distance. It was different; not a car or truck, and it wasn't coming at us, but *by* us, and it grew louder. Then there came the long, echoing hoot of a train whistle. It moved slowly, and I knew enough about trains to know they blew their whistles when approaching stations they don't stop at.

I shudder to remember this, and my bodiless body goes electric, as if my senses blow wide open. There are rails near cabins, near a bridge, near a train depot, near a gas station.

The train was long. It dragged a lot of cars. They clicked heavily over the point where sections of rail join. There wouldn't be a passenger train that late at night with so many cars in that part of the state, so it had to be a freight train.

Straining my ears, I tried to count the cars. I couldn't, but when I heard each car clunk over track with a sound that didn't seem laid on solid ground, I knew the train was crossing a bridge.

The neighborhood forms in my mind. I have it in front of me as I fly back in the car.

"Look for a train bridge," I tell Matt. *"Some cabins near a railroad station and probably a river or a creek."*

Meally?

"Yes, really. Look for it!"

He goes back to his phone and pretty quickly eliminates three of the four places. A cottage park called Four Pines Motor Cabins is near a station and a pair of bridges, one a road bridge, the other for rail. It's so near where we're driving at that moment, it scares me.

"Dad," he starts, "I . . . I . . ."

My body shifts suddenly to the left, as if we're turning right, but Dad is driving dead straight. *"Matt . . . take a right. Matt, tell Dad to take a right. Soon . . . soon . . . Matt, now!"*

"Dad, turn right!"

"Matt, what?"

"Turn!" Matt grabs the wheel and yanks it toward him.

"What the hell! Matt!"

The car skids right, then bounces onto a short road, and

DENIS EVER AFTER

Dad angrily jerks the car to a stop. "Matt! What in the world are you doing?"

"Denis was taken here! I know it. They brought him here! There's a bridge and gravel—"

"And train tracks—"

"And railroad tracks. Dad, you have to believe me!"

Our father's face reddens in anger and confusion. I glimpse another face in his for an instant before it vanishes. It's an old woman's face. White hair.

"Matt, come on. This is crazy. What's really going on?"

"Tell him, Matt, just tell him I'm here."

I know this will hurt me, spreading myself wide. You can't haunt more and more people, set up shop here, then waltz back to Port Haven like you never left. I already feel how haunting thickens you. It leaves a mark. It shows. It's like any habit. You drink too much and you die early. The more combat missions you go on, the better chance you'll die. I won't be able to stop my rush to vanishing, but Dad needs it, Matt needs it, Mom needs it, maybe the most. So, yeah.

Matt's jammed his eyes shut, tears rushing out despite himself.

Dad reaches across the seat to him, takes his shaking hand. "Listen, I get it. Maybe this was a bad idea, like Mom warned us, but something's going on with you. You have to give me some credit, Matt. A clue so I can try to help."

"It's okay," I whisper to Matt. *"Tell Dad. I'll be fine."*

I won't be.

"I've been kind of . . . seeing Denis. And hearing him. It's why I was a jerk at school."

Dad sets his jaw, swallows. "Where?" he says gently, like a social worker or a teacher. "Matt, where do you see Denis?"

I wait for Matt to turn his head to me. I shift to catch the moonlight, like I did in his room that first night, so I can show myself to Dad.

Matt breathes in, then out, twice. "In my mind," he says. "I hear his voice, too, telling me stuff. I don't know how. Maybe because we're twins? We've known each other since even before you and Mom did."

"Matt, really, there's no . . ." He stops, readjusts what he's thinking. "Twins? I don't know."

"The two creepy men I remembered tonight at Funland, they took Denis in their car. He couldn't move, he was tied up in the trunk. They came here. He's telling me this stuff in my mind. It's his voice, I know it. The men stayed in a cabin. Cabin seven."

Dad breathes out a long breath. He stares straight ahead. "I saw," he says. "I saw my grandmother once. I mean, I didn't, but I thought I did. After she died."

Matt sniffs up. "What? Really? When?"

A shake of the head. "Last year."

"You never said anything."

"Of course not. She's been gone for, what, ten years? But

there she was in our garage in Buckwood, talking to me. I hadn't stayed in touch, really. And, now that I remember it, it was more like she was yelling at me. She doesn't mince words, that woman. She didn't."

"What did she tell you?"

Dad shrugs. "Something about him. My father. It wasn't real, of course. It was just me imagining the whole thing. I don't think about her much, really. That's why it was strange."

Matt glances at me for an instant. "That's amazing. I guess that's what I feel with Denis."

"Well, I made the mistake of telling your mother. That's why she secretly thinks I'm a little *off*." More deep breaths as Dad looks down the road and then at Matt. "So. Cabin seven, huh?"

"Or maybe a cottage. I'm not sure, but it's right around here. We're close. I feel it."

Dad looks at Matt silently for the longest time. Their eyes are fixed on each other, and I see in Matt's that he completely believes me, loves me, and he's doing everything he can to spark these feelings over to our father. Dad's confused, his brain spinning wildly, but a sliver of light suddenly passes between them, and it's as if a layer of skin falls away.

"Matt, you *have* been different lately. Maybe since you found the police file, and I know that's partly my fault. But sometimes, it feels like you're blanking out on me, you know?"

"Blanking out?"

"Going somewhere in your mind. I do it too. Mom's not the bad guy here, but she notices. And she worries about you. I do too."

Matt swallows hard, trying to think of something to say. Finally, he shrugs a little. "I'm sorry?"

"No, don't be sorry. Matt, we're just concerned, that's all."

"I'm okay, Dad. I just feel these things. And if today is it, no more hunting for clues after we get back, then let's do this and see if anything happens and if we find something out. Okay?"

Dad puts his hand on the shift and turns his face to the road ahead. It's shaded with long patches of moonlight pocking the pavement. "We're already so late, but . . ." He locks the shift into drive. "Let's see where this leads. Then we go home. Got it?"

"Yes. Absolutely. Thanks, Dad."

He drives slowly down the road, which rumbles across a low bridge, where a second road crosses it. They stay straight, then right, left, left, nearly into a stretch of ragged fencing, when Dad spots a sudden break in the fence, and he slides onto a gravel path, deeply rutted. He stops the car. The road ends in a field of tall grass and weeds.

No cabins.

"But I thought . . . ," Matt says, flicking his eyes back at me.

"Matt, it's okay," Dad says quietly. "You want to solve this. So do I. But maybe we've gone as far as we can, and there just isn't any more."

They both sit there without saying anything for a minute, maybe longer. Then, slowly, as if he doesn't want to, Dad shifts into reverse. Looking both ways, he drives back a few feet over the ruts, then suddenly slams the brakes.

"Holy crow, Matt!"

Far across the field to the left, an old sign tilts under a sputtering spotlight:

FOUR PINES MOTOR CABINS

30

AT CABIN SEVEN

Dad grips the wheel so hard his knuckles turn white, and he wrestles it, as if he wants to tear the thing right off the steering post. "What the heck? Is this some kind of prank?"

Matt shakes his head in disbelief. "I . . . I've never been here before. How would I know?"

Staring at the sign, Dad spins through a world of questions in his head, one after another after another, until he rejects the idea that Matt is trying to trick him. That would just be cruel. Matt is not like that. He's suffering too. All this is what Dad thinks.

Finally, he lets his hands fall into his lap, tilts his head, looks out the rearview.

"Well, it's actually not on this road. It's got to be on the one we passed just after the bridge. You got it wrong by one street, and I nearly crashed, but you found it. You actually found it."

"I got it wrong by one street," Matt repeats, swatting the space I occupy.

"Missed me."

Unable to turn around on the narrow road, Dad backs out to where the second road crosses this one. He drives slowly along it. It's a mess, barely paved, but it widens as we near the cabin park. Seeing it, I become heavy and my veins flood with sadness. The place is pretty much as I had imagined from the trunk five years ago. A wide arc of identical, gloomy clapboard cottages with a drab office building at the foot of the flickering sign.

"Matt, from here on, maybe don't repeat everything I tell you. Dad's already way suspicious. Just play dumb about some things. Which I know is easy for you."

He swats the air again.

Dad parks outside the office to talk to the desk manager while Matt and I get out to look around. There's not a lot to see. Four Pines is at the edge of a field of high grass and overgrown weeds. Maybe it was once on a well-traveled route, but it sure isn't anymore.

We walk down the rutted path to cabin seven. No surprise, it actually *is* at the end of a lane of one- and two-room cottages like I guessed from the trunk. Like the others, number seven is white with red trim and a peaked roof. The paint is peeling, baring warped gray wood beneath.

"These have to be way old," Matt says. "Same era as the Dipper?"

I almost snicker, but don't. "One of the thousand, thousand threads."

There's a minivan parked at the side of number seven, and a towel drying on the back of a red wooden chair in front. Two beach chairs are folded up against the railing that surrounds the front porch. There's no beach anywhere near here. It smells like gasoline and popcorn.

"People are in cabin seven right now," Matt says. "How weird."

A silver-haired woman in a blue dress from one of the other cabins walks under an overhead light to the manager's hut, her low heels grinding carefully in the gravel. She's cursing to herself, and her choice language takes me back five years, to what I heard in that trunk.

Sandbag and One-Eye had started going at it again near the car, but it was softer now, as if they didn't want anyone to hear. It may have been deep in the night.

In his nasally way, One-Eye came out with, "Momma-May's just too sick. Even if we get money for the kid, the home'll know we got it of a sudden and call the cops."

"They won't find out nothing. For a brother you're a joke."

"Well, there's too many things wrong about your 'plan,' and I ain't doing it. Heck with this. Heck with you always hittin' me, too."

Sandbag swore at him for "being a coward, just like in Eye-Rack" and smacked him again.

One-Eye stomped away. He stomped away from the car, from the cabin, from me, saying, "You finish up this mess. I don't care how. I'm hopping the next freight to the Lincoln. Meet me if you want to, I don't care."

And One-Eye's footsteps receded in the gravel until Sandbag slammed his fists, both of them, hard on the trunk. It boomed in my ears. He kept doing it again and again. "You're dead now, pixie!" he hissed. "You hear me? *Deeeaaaad.*" He stretched out the last word like a song lyric.

After One-Eye left I didn't hear his voice again. In fact, nothing happened for a long time. No cars came into Four Pines. As starving as I was, aching all over, I fell asleep in the trunk.

When I woke up—this was Monday—acid was burning a hole in my stomach. I was shivering. I didn't bother holding it in, and I peed again, which was warm, then cold. There was frost on the ceiling of the trunk.

The sun couldn't have been up yet, I reasoned, because

I still heard the hum of the lights over the porches. A cabin door opened and shut with a soft click. A single set of footsteps approached across the gravel. The back door of the car eased open and stuff was thrown inside. Sandbag's gear. A few seconds later the trunk lid popped open over me.

I still couldn't see, but I smelled cold fresh air and felt no sun on my limbs. It was still dark, maybe overcast. I tried to shout. My voice was muffled.

"We're going for a teensy ride now," Sandbag hissed. "Don't make no more messes in Jenny!"

Then I sensed him lean over and crack me on the side of my head.

I just had time to realize that he had called the car Jenny, when everything was black again.

31

I'M SORRY FOR YOUR LOSS

Dad tramps down past the cabins, whispering into his phone—to Mom?—then stops short to end the conversation before he walks over to Matt, rolling his shoulders.

"So the joker in the office laughed when I asked about five years ago. 'Like we keep records of that stuff,' he said. And he didn't actually say 'stuff.' But he doesn't 'give a good gosh darn' if we ask the guests to look inside. Also not what he said. I wanted to smack him. You want to come with me?"

Matt stares at the cabin, as if he's trying to etch it in his mind, then shakes his head. "No."

Dad nods. He gets it. He climbs the steps and knocks on the door.

"*Look, Matt,*" I whisper. "*One-Eye left me with Sandbag*

and took the train out of here. Monday morning Sandbag drove me off again."

The door opens and Dad is invited inside.

Matt frowns. "So you were never inside the cabin anyway? You were in the trunk all night?"

"In the car all night. I was hurting everywhere and kept wiggling my tooth, not thinking that if it actually came out, I'd be in trouble. I had to keep swallowing puke or I'd suffocate. I was starving. I went . . . I wet my pants a couple of times. Then Sandbag knocked me out again."

Matt's eyes water up. "I'm so sorry, Den. I'm so sorry you were in there. . . ."

These are the times I wish I could just put my hand on his shoulder. I try to now. He can't feel anything, but he leans into it, as if he does.

"You don't remember any more?" he whispers. "Like where Sandbag took you? Maybe not Gettysburg yet, but back over the bridge? Somewhere you saw the tall thing in your eye?"

I shrug. "One-Eye said he was taking the train 'to Lincoln,' wherever that is."

"I'll check. On the train line?" While Dad is in the cabin, he opens his phone. "Uh-oh, a text. It's from Mom. To call her."

"In a minute," I say. "The car is bothering me, too. Sandbag called it Jenny. But if it was stolen, I mean, who gives a name to a stolen car? I don't know if Jenny even *is* the Honda. I never saw it. It doesn't fit somehow."

"Please," he groans. "Not *two* cars."

I feel my empty stomach of five years ago. "Find anything?"

"Lincoln is in Allegheny County. It's not far away, I guess, but it's not on the same train route, so I don't know how he was planning on—"

"Wait! Not Lincoln. *The* Lincoln. One-Eye was going to *the* Lincoln. Search on that."

More tapping and swiping and head shaking, until finally, "Ha, found it! The Lincoln Inn, on Broad Street in Evanton. Right near the tracks, no more than a half hour from here—"

Dad steps out onto the cabin porch. "Thank you. So much."

"I'm sorry for your loss," a young man says from inside. Two small boys come up behind him and look out. They must be four or under. "Are you the twin?" their father says to Matt.

"Yes."

"I'm sorry you lost your brother. Gosh, if either of these . . ." He puts his hands on his sons' heads, as if to protect them.

Matt purses his lips tight, reminding me of the way Mom

looks when she can't say what she's feeling. He can only nod before he has to turn away. We walk slowly to the car, and it's minutes before he can find it in himself to speak.

"So. Dad. What now?"

"I'll phone Ed Sparn when we get home. He's the detective. You'll see his name in the file. Look, I believe you, and I don't know how you're finding these things, but after five years, this probably won't go very far, you know? In the meantime . . ." And I can suddenly tell Dad is working on something in his mind and trying to find a way to make it sound normal. He finally gives up. "Look, Matt, I don't want you to be surprised when we get home"—he checks his phone for the time—"but Mommy's going to tell you that . . . we're going to counseling."

"Counseling? For what? You and Mom? Dad, no. You guys are okay—"

"No, Matt. Not just us. All three of us."

"Me? Why?"

"For this. For Denis, for what it's doing to us. It's not just you. I've been stuck on this for years. I can't do that. It's hurting us. It's really hurting you, whether you know it or not, though I suspect you do. You're hearing things, seeing things. We're doing this trip now, you and me, because, well, I want to. But your mother is right. This is serious—"

"Dad, no. I'm okay. Really. Let's just keep going—"

"Matt, wait. It might actually help us," I interrupt him, and he flicks his eyes toward me. *"If you agree to this, let them get all questiony with you, you can start asking them things."*

"See, like just then," Dad says. "You sort of zombied out on me."

Matt tries to object, but his thoughts and whatever he feels are caught between me and Dad. "Yeah, but . . ." He seems suddenly to lose air. "Who? And when?"

"Monday. After school. I don't know who the counselor is. Mommy found somebody."

Matt breathes out the last little bit of oxygen. "Okay. Okay. I'll go. I'll be real open and say lots of stuff, and all that, but there's one last stop." His finger shakes as he swipes his phone open at the map. "Evanton. The Lincoln Inn. It's between here and home. You have to take me."

Dad leans over Matt's phone. "You think Denis was taken there, to this inn?"

"Not exactly . . ." Then a sudden spray of white sparks fall from him, from his face, like he's shedding water, or crying, and he covers his eyes with the palms of his hands. "Denis was kept in a trunk. He was beaten up. He peed on himself. He . . ."

"Matt."

And Matt falls to his knees, or almost, but Dad picks him up, holds him up, barely able to do that himself, and I want to fly away. I shouldn't be here with them. Matt begged me to come, but now I see what I'm doing to him. Dad said they're all hurting. Yeah, and *I'm* the one hurting them. Me in the past. Me now.

"*Matt, I should go—*"

"So let's find this place," Dad says, patting Matt on the back, leading him to the car. "An inn, huh? Final last stop."

"*Matt, really. I should go back.*"

But the way Matt jumps into his seat and slams the door, I wonder if he heard me.

We drive on.

Twenty minutes later we're stopping at an intersection, where one slow route crosses another, and I don't know, maybe it's the road signs, pointing to different towns, but I suddenly remember Kittanning and that Trey couldn't discover anything much about it.

Neither Mom nor Dad lived there in the census years. But as Dad punches the gas to start up from the stop, I nudge Matt to ask him.

"*As long as he's here with you, maybe he'll tell you.*"

Matt sucks in a breath. "Dad, have you ever been to Kittanning?"

"Kittanning. Kittanning. I don't think so. If I was, I don't remember it."

"What's there?"

He shrugs. "I don't know. The usual. It's about an hour

from us. From Buckwood. Why?"

"I just, I don't know. Do you know anyone who lives there? Or who used to?"

Dad thinks about that for a mile or so before he shakes his head. "I can't think of a soul. And I'm not sure I ever actually passed through it. Why are you asking?"

"Funny name, I guess."

Dad laughs. "Oh, Pennsylvania's got them. Punxsutawney, Petrolia, Coraopolis, Zelienople. I lived in Zelie with your great-grandmother." He laughs again, only it's a cold laugh. "I don't think much about those times anymore."

And that's it from Dad. He doesn't say any more about the past, and Matt doesn't press it.

"If that was GeeGee's junk in the suitcase, she knows about Kittanning. The vaccination slips, remember?"

"Of course I poo."

It's then I realize I haven't thought of GeeGee for hours.

Less than fifteen minutes after this conversation, we are there, rolling slowly in the car on a dark street in downtown Evanton. The nearer we get, the more my temples begin to throb.

The Lincoln Inn is a five-story pile of crumbling brick and stone surrounded by wire fences and draped with nets to catch falling debris. The word DEMO is sprayed on the boarded windows on each side of the main doors, which you can barely read since the sun is gone and the streetlight in front of the place is, of course, out.

The instant I see it, I know it's what I was warned about. An encampment, the souls of the lost trapped inside a hotel of misery. Also, I hear wailing.

"Looks empty," Matt says.

"Yeah, except no."

"What do you expect to find here?" Dad asks.

Matt shrugs, then half turns to me. "Yeah, what?"

"Souls," I say. "Maybe they know something."

Exiting the car, Dad scouts the street, which isn't deserted, but isn't exactly alive, either. A car passes. Minutes later, a police cruiser rolls by. Then nothing for minutes.

"Tell him to drive to the back of the building."

Matt does, and Dad slowly pulls down the side street to the rear. Security fence wires that off too. The rear facade is black, the windows glassless. Three pickups are parked up on the sidewalk, several cars, and one motorcycle with a tarp on it. A backhoe sits chained on a trailer.

Dad sizes it up. "Too bad. No one to talk to. We can take a picture at least."

Matt gets out. I do too, when there is the sudden whoop of a siren. Dad turns, looks both ways.

"Dang! We're on a one-way street!"

185

"*Go! Go!*" I yell to Matt, and he follows me down the street.

"Matt, get back here!" Dad yells, but freezes when the police car pulls up.

We are away in a shot. The officer exits the cruiser. Matt hurries behind the trailer to where a pile of wooden pallets is stacked inside the fence. "Should we try to get in this way?"

"Kind of your choice," I say. "I can float in anywhere."

He gives me a face. "Lucky."

"Said no one, ever. Hurry up."

Looking both ways, he grabs on to the wire with both hands and scrambles up, toeing his sneakers into the holes. Once he's at the crest, he swings both feet around and lowers himself onto the top pallet, then jumps to the ground.

The wailing from inside the building spikes, and I feel a rush of cold air from the souls gathered there. I don't want to go in, don't want to see a pack of stranded laggards, but the purpose of this is to solve my stupid death so my family can stay together. While I rip apart.

But no, it's fine. It's all fine.

There isn't much of a lock system, and before you know it we're inside the dank, dark lobby that smells overwhelmingly of mold and rats. Matt has trouble seeing me as his eyes adjust, but I have no trouble seeing the other ghosts. Dozens drift around the lobby, wandering among the columns, stuck between here and where they're supposed to be, having stayed too long as minglers, sliced in half so many times they can no longer connect the parts of themselves.

The thought of it makes me ill right down the middle.

"Anyone here?" Matt whispers.

"Oh, yeah."

32

THASS ME. I'M MELROSE.

One spirit, an older lady in a neat green dress, sits on a ratty old lobby sofa, surrounded by photo albums. She jumps up when she sees me.

"Qiang! Oh, Qiang! It's so good to finally see you. Qiang, you've grown so tall!"

"I'm . . . I'm not Qiang," I tell her.

"No, no. I would know my nephew anywhere."

"I'm really sorry. I'm not Qiang. Maybe he's not here . . . yet."

She blinks, hustles back to the sofa for a photo album. "But I'm sure it's . . ." She looks at a picture, then does a double take at me. "Oh, I see . . . it's not you. Qiang is . . . I've been waiting so long. . . ."

"Your nephew ain't coming, lady! I tode you!" shouts a raspy voice from the darkness off the lobby. "He don't remember you, why should he? He moved three years ago to Hongo Kongo. I seen him move. *You* seen him move. Buh-bye!"

"That's not nice!" I call back. "And it's racist, too."

"Come here and say that!"

I don't.

Shaking, the woman thrusts her hands to her face and shouts so loud that Matt jerks back.

"We got a fader!" somebody yells, and instantly, spirits swarm out of the shadows like a flock of vultures. But as swift as the souls mass, what happens to the woman seems to unfold in slow motion. She goes rigid and lets out a wail that shakes the room. Her eyes grow huge in her face. The mass of heavy souls in the lobby is suffocating me, but Matt has a different reaction.

"I . . . hear something. Denis, I . . ."

"Her," I tell him. "A soul. Her nephew forgot her. She's dying again."

"I feel them around us! Hundreds. They're staring . . . gawking at her!"

More than gawking, the souls cheer the woman on, like crazed bystanders at a schoolyard fight. The poor lady begins to rock on her heels, screaming and blubbering, until with one great wail, she comes apart. Her face splits, her chest breaks open wide, her whole body comes apart down the middle with a sound like the ripping of heavy fabric that sprays something wet on my cheeks. Inside her is emptiness, a black nothing. The crowd roars vulgarly, as the nothing pours from the gap and folds around her, until suddenly, shriekingly, she is gone. Gone. Not there.

There is nothing where she just stood.

"She mingled too much!" one old man howls, forgetting that the same thing must happen to him and to all of them. But no, it was someone else this time. That's all that matters.

"You're next, sonny!" a young woman snarls to someone.

"Nuh-uh, you!"

"You're both next!" calls a third.

And more like that. I'm sick in my chest and throat, I feel like vomiting.

Matt wears an expression of terror on his face. Of terror and crushing sadness. "She . . . exploded, didn't she?" he whispers. "She did. I know she did. Denis, is that what you . . ."

He can't finish.

I close my eyes, see only darkness inside. When I open them the crowd of souls has dispersed, sullen now that the show is over. Only one figure remains, a strange, wavering shadow of a man. He is very thin, his face is sort of squashed at an angle, and he hops, almost, on one foot, over to us. The leg? Again? I wonder what it all means. He wears what was once a camouflage jacket but is shreds now. A newspaper is folded high in his armpit.

"Kid, kid, kid," he rasps. "You're new here."

Matt's eyes are riveted on the approaching shadow, sensing it more than seeing it. As much as he is able to, he tries to nudge me with his elbow, then backs away, though the ghost is clearly not interested in him. He shuffles up and pushes the newspaper at me.

"Read it out."

We hear the police car roar loudly down the street outside. I take the yellowed paper.

"Matt!" Dad calls from outside the building. "Are you in there?"

"It's the *Butler Eagle*," the ghost slurs. "Five years ago. Page nine. Read it out."

Even before I read the date, I realize I've seen the paper before. It's one Matt had in his room when I first visited him. The headline screams at me.

COMMUNITY MOURNS LOST TWIN OF PERRY STUDENT

It's dated the Saturday after Thanksgiving, three days after they found me. I turn to page nine. The small photograph of a face above the fold has been thumbed so often the ink has worn away. I can't make it out. Next to it is a short article. "Local Hit-and-Run Victim Dies."

"Read it out," the shadow says a third time, shifting from one foot to the damaged other one. "They won't anymore. They say they tired. Read it out." The voice grates in my head. His throat has obviously been damaged, but there is something odd about it that pinches my memory as I read.

"'A former city resident struck by a hit-and-run driver Tuesday evening, November 20, at the corner of North Jackson and Stewart Streets, died Friday morning of his injuries.'"

"Tuesday," Matt whispers. "The same day you died."

I keep reading. "'Melrose Tibbs, aged thirty-one, had been in a coma at UPMC Passavant Hospital since the incident. Tibbs was a native of Lyndora, and had resided at various addresses in Petrolia and New Castle since returning from service in Iraq in 2009. He is survived by his mother, Maybelline, currently of Buckwood, but predeceased by his father, Macy Tibbs, a decorated veteran of the Korean War, formerly of Coraopolis. The status of an older brother, Maywell Tibbs, is unknown. The hit-and-run accident remains unsolved and is now considered a homicide.'"

"Thass me. I'm Melrose." And his voice stabs at me again. "But it ain't a homicide. It truly was an accident. I was drinking and fell into that road going from there to here, which is where I am living now." The man's face bears a red scar from his forehead straight down to his chin. "It was the night it snowed. Hadn't snowed before that."

He lifts his face to me, and I see where his right eye should be is open and dry, a hole.

"You looking at my eye. I had a glass eye from the war, but I lost it that night." He laughs. "It fell into the drain when the car hit me."

I am nearly too choked to speak. "You!"

"I know which drain, too, but I can't get it now. It sitting down there just looking up at the sky forever. Funny, ain't it? If people knew they was being watched by a dead eye! I come back down here from the Haven to look for it. Three, four times already. But now I'm afraid to go back up there. I'd rip apart!"

"You!" I say again.

"Denis?" Matt whispers, putting his hand on my arm, maybe feeling something. "Denis?"

"You kidnapped me!" I yell.

The man steps back, shaking his ruined head. "Who? Me? Naw! I died."

"Before you died! You kidnapped me at the amusement park and stuffed me in your trunk. Jenny. Jenny was the name of your car! I was at Funland and you kidnapped me from my family. Then you killed me! You and that bum with the sandbag belly! That creep beat me!"

He snatches back the newspaper I'm shaking at him.

"Naw! Thass my brother, Maywell. I never beat you. I died. I'm dead now."

"Four Pines Cabins! You took me there in your trunk, then you killed me!"

"What? Naw," he says softly, looking me over. "I was at Four Pines? What was I like?"

"You killed me! That's what you were like. You're a murderer!"

He's shaking his head more and more violently. "You got that wrong. I never . . ."

"You killed me and took me to Gettysburg."

"Gettysburg? Ha! I ain't been to Gettysburg never." He seems to remember something. "Maywell took you away from that cabin. Thass what. He took you away from that cabin."

"Liar! Where? Where did he take me?"

He eyes me, afraid. "I don't know. But that was the plan. We were going to find out from the news who you were and get us money for Momma-May. . . ."

"Ransom!" Matt says suddenly. "I heard him. I knew it!"

"But I didn't like Maywell's plan and left you there and came to here instead. Maywell never came here. He took you away, but I don't know where—" He seems suddenly taken with a new thought. "Maybe he drowned you! Maywell drowned a dog once in a lake when we were small."

"A lake?"

"He must of got mad and drowned you in the lake too. Like that dog."

"The lake? What lake?" I scream.

"Maywell wasn't right after Eye-Rack, not that he was much right before. But we couldn't work. No one hired us. Twice times I stopped him killing himself."

"Tell me! What. Lake!"

Matt sees me quivering. "What is he saying?"

"Are you sure your brother drowned me in a lake? Are you *sure*?"

"Aw, I don't know. I was dead, or nearly. I'm sorry for what I did. It was for Momma-May, but it wasn't right, and I'm sorry. I know I did bad things. Please forgive me, please—"

All at once, he starts to quiver like the woman did. He grabs his face and screams. "Ohhh!"

"Melrose?" a deep voice shouts out from the back of the lobby. "Melrose! Stop that!"

And he stops. Melrose Tibbs stops screaming and splitting. He tears his hands away from his face and looks behind him at a man staggering across the lobby to us. By his age and the way Melrose hops to greet him, hands clasping, embracing, I guess that it's his father, Macy Tibbs. They hold each other close. Melrose tries to calm himself in the old man's arms.

"Leave the poor boy alone," the man says to me. "He was wrong, so wrong, but he's apologized now. You can see how he's suffered. He'll come and join us now. He's allowed to. Melrose, leave this place and come home now."

"Aww, Daddy. I don't want to split. I'm sorry. I really am."

"I know you are, Melrose, and please stop that silly way of speaking you and your brother picked up in the army. You're from Pennsylvania. Young man, please let Melrose be. He's suffered much in his young life, but he's no killer. He's sorry. Now, son, I think it's time you and I left this place."

"It's over, then?" Melrose says. "No ripping up?"

"Let him rip!" some soul says from behind the registration desk, and the shades begin to gather excitedly again.

"No!" Macy says sharply. "No! He will not rip. Not if I am with him—"

"Rip, rip, rip!"

Macy Tibbs swings around angrily and fixes his eyes on the greedy shadows. "A soul who loves him shall keep him safe. It's being forgotten that kills. I haven't forgotten my loved one!"

The excited voices go quiet, and Macy Tibbs slips a ghostly Pirates cap on his son's head. "Just follow me, now, Melrose. Once more into the razor, then no more." Then turning to me, he says, "I'm sorry, young man, I really am. You seem nice, but no more, I beg you. Melrose is sorry. I'll usher him home now."

Stunned, I back away, gasping at this bizarre scene of a father and his son. *A soul who loves him shall keep him safe.* When I finally turn to Matt, he's shaking and crying. He's seen some, but he's heard more, and it's terrified him.

Boards are breaking across the lobby now. In unison, the ghosts swivel around to see my father, tramping across the floor, mad as a hornet.

"Matt, get over here! You're lucky the police had to take off. Out of here. Now! *Now!*"

Even as Melrose and his father fade quietly across the room in front of me, the other ghosts implore us to remain, reaching out their bony dead hands, pleading.

They even go after Dad—"Pity me! Save me! Remember me!"—but Dad doesn't hear and Matt doesn't tell him.

We tear out the back doors into the street. A stark wind barrels down over us. I wipe my cheek, damp from that lady's insides. *"Matt, I'm worried. I have to check if GeeGee's okay."*

"What?"

"Get in the car, Matt. Come on," Dad growls as they make their way out the back of the building. "This will be part of counseling, too. You know that."

"Denis, please don't leaf me!" he pleads, sounding almost like the ghosts now.

But I have to. Dad has scared me by blocking GeeGee out of his mind. Matt scares me more by remembering her only from a photo he once saw. Her hand has never been on his forehead, he never heard her gentle voice or saw what I see in her eyes.

"I have to go back!" I say as Dad hustles Matt into the car.

"Bub the therapiss! You have to be there!"

"Sixty-dollar ticket!" Dad snarls, jumping into his seat and starting the car with a roar.

"I need to go back. I'm scared about her. You and Trey find this killer lake—"

"Where do we even fart looking? Transylvania has millions of latkes!"

"It probably does, but look for a lake near any of the places we've been to."

Finding me in the light of a streetlamp, he says, "Hairy back. Good duck, bra."

And I wonder if he'll ever get it.

"Good duck to you, too. I'll be back as soon as I can!"

33

IF ANYBODY ASKS YOU WHERE I'M GOING

The screams of that poor woman and Melrose Tibbs
sear into my brain, and I can't stop thinking how Dad said
GeeGee came to him last year. She can't be doing that. What
if she tries to come again?

She might do that. I can imagine her coming here. But if
she does, an old lady in the razor . . .

The thought of what might happen turns me to ice.

Closing my eyelids tight until all light turns purple
behind them, I conjure the burning blade. Easy enough. It's
always there in my head, like that high-pitched ringing in old
people's ears.

The razor shreds me far more than before. I try to push
through and get it over with, but there's no hurrying and no

lessening the pain. When I'm finally back in the gray room, I imagine blood pooling on the floor, like on that bloody street in Valdosta, but, no, it's just the red pain inside me.

I need to check on her, and I quickly hike down from the woods to her house.

GeeGee, I say in my mind, *GeeGee*, over and over until I finally call out, "GeeGee!" like I called for Matt and my parents at Funland. Heading directly to the street where she lives, I see the sun is not yet down, but the air is gray and cold on my skin. The horizon is a dark smudge. I keep going, able to pick up speed as the pain of the razor lessens. I'm nearly there, three streets away, then two, then somehow I make a wrong turn.

I make a wrong turn.

After five years in Port Haven, I mistake the way to her house.

Trying to place myself on the grid of streets, I pause on the sidewalk and glance back to the hills, which are fogged over, too. "I've gone too far," I say to myself. I backtrack and finally spot a squat blue house. GeeGee's bungalow is around the corner from a blue house.

But as I approach the corner, I feel suddenly as if someone's punched the air out of me. I'm not sure if I'm supposed to turn right or left. I feel off-center. Have I been sliced down the middle too often? What did he say, Macy Tibbs? It's being forgotten that kills? I know that! And I haven't forgotten my loved one. But have I spent too much time below? Have I done something bad? He warned me I might get confused, the writer . . . white hair . . . notebook . . . he did.

I shut my eyes. No, no. I'm just confused. Like when you go too quickly from light into darkness, like Matt at the encampment hotel. Your eyes are shocked by the contrast. You're surprised, and it takes a few seconds to adjust.

My left eyebrow stings. I rub away the pain.

Never mind. I'll find her. GeeGee. And I'll tell her everything Matt and I discovered below, and she'll tell me the secrets she knows.

Spying her bungalow at last, my heart skips a beat. It looks exactly as I remember, although a new plant sits near the front steps, a red flowering thing I've never seen before. No, no. The problem was only the couple of days I spent below. It's the earthly things I discovered about my death that are throwing me off now.

I'm through the gate into GeeGee's yard. It's neat, recently mowed and trimmed.

"GeeGee!"

Of course she's not in her yard or on the porch, it's too cold. Even so, I call her again.

"GeeGee."

The front door. It's painted dark green now, not the color it was, though I can't recall what color it used to be. I tell myself I like it and will compliment her when she opens it.

I hop up the steps, letting my feet pound on the boards to show that I'm here but also that I'm happy to be back and that I have things to tell her and ask her.

I knock. "GeeGee!"

Hearing no footsteps inside, I twist the knob. It's locked. I tap again with my knuckles, harder this time. The door is tacky, the paint is fresh. I peek in the narrow windows flanking the door, salute with both hands to keep out the light, though it's already overcast. The foyer is dark, there's a gleam of polish on the side table in the entry hall and on the floorboards. The carpet is freshly crisscrossed by a vacuum. My heart pounds. I knock a third time. No answer.

I think of the beach club. Maybe she's there reading or playing cards. Yes, of course. Why did I come here? That's where she is. I should have gone there first!

After trying the knob a final time, I hurry down to the beach. Ella or Ellen is not on the sand, watching for boats, which I put down to it being cold, but even the ball courts are vacant, and they never are. The grotto is deserted and cold. I run to the beach club. Its long porch is empty except for a single card table at the far end.

In the dim light I see figures. A flash of silver white hair. Not GeeGee, though. It's him. The writer. Russo.

"Russo!" I trot up the stairs to him. "Russo! I'm back. It seems like forever. Do you know where GeeGee is?"

He looks up with sleepy eyes. He's got an open notebook in his lap, but he isn't holding a pen and isn't playing cards, though a man with a strange flip of pink hair shuffles them repeatedly.

"The name is Russell," Russo says, and when I apologize, he adds, "Your features are . . . not quite aligned."

At first I think he means the gap in my eyebrow, but when I touch my forehead and chin, I feel a faint line like an old scar. "Never mind me. Russell, have you seen GeeGee today? I can't find her."

"I haven't seen anyone." Russell lowers his head to his notebook. "Certainly not today."

Next to the lady with the big black medical sunglasses sits a young guy rubbing his spine from side to side on the back of GeeGee's chair. His eyes shine like glass. His shoes and pant legs are wet.

The man with the swirl of pink hair has begun dealing—*flap, flap, flap*—and glaring at each player as if he expects a reaction to the cards he's snapping on the tabletop, but only some cards are faceup. He tilts his head to me, but not his eyes. "This GeeGee? Is she tall? Who is she?"

"What? My great-grandmother. You know her, you play cards with her—"

"Now listen, little boy," the pink-haired man snarls, "I know who I know and I don't know who I don't know and don't tell me otherwise! I'm simply asking, is she tall?"

I feel light-headed, dizzy. "No. She's short. Slight. White hair."

"Goodness!" he says. "She reminds me of my mother. You're not looking for my *mother*?"

"No! I'm looking for GeeGee! She smells like fresh oranges. She plays cards with you—"

"Oh, I don't think she does!" Pink Hair deals two more cards, scowling at the other players, who don't return his glances. "And I'm not sure I like oranges, boy."

I try to calm my heart. "Seriously, no one has seen my GeeGee?"

The young guy grunts under his breath, and Russell acts as if he's not even here, pretending to scribble in his book with his fingertip. The whole place has gone insane.

"Come on, all of you! I need to talk to GeeGee! And who is this new guy in her chair?"

The man gawks at me. His mouth moves as if forming words, but nothing comes out, and he doesn't stop clawing at his back. Russell appears strangely ashamed. He looks me up and down and something moves in his expression. "Come over here," he says. He rises from his seat at the table, and the man with pink hair snarls as we steal away to a pair of chairs overlooking the sea.

A ceiling lamp flickers over us.

Russell frowns at his finger, dipped between the pages

of his notebook. "I sometimes make notes about people. For my . . . well, I don't know why, exactly, I just do."

"You're writing a book," I say, dredging that up from my memory.

"If you say so." He opens to the page and studies, as if he's trying to read a foreign language. "Now, could your name be . . ." And seconds go by as he tries to read, like those that lapsed when I tried to remember his name for Matt. ". . . could your name be . . . Denis?"

"Yes! You wrote about me? I was seven when I got here. The police say I died on November twentieth, five years ago. It snowed. They found my body at a monument at Gettysburg."

He closes the notebook for a moment. "Ah, a battlefield. There are so many. In rooms, in houses, on streets, in the sand and dirt. I like to say—or was it someone else?—that one tiny moment is just one of a thousand, thousand threads that twine together to make every one of us who we are and who we aren't."

"Isn't that what your book is about?" I tap the notebook, wanting him to open it. "People?"

"Possibly." He holds it to the lamplight again. "And your person, her name?"

"GeeGee. I told you. I think she's gone back too many times. She visited my father. And my grandfather before that. You have to remember her, Russell, you have to."

"But I rather think it's because *you* didn't, that she's not here. Perhaps it was you alone who kept her here. And you left, so . . ."

"What? No, it's my family down there, it's their fault."

"Is it? We like to think so, but we don't really know. We don't know how it all works. After all, *we* forget the living, too, don't we? The living and the not-living forget one another. No sense in staying *anywhere*, once that happens. Besides, you forgot her, too, didn't you?"

"Russell, no. No. I didn't forget, not all the way. I came back to ask GeeGee stuff and to tell her what I discovered. Not only about my death, but other things, too. Someone told me it's messy there, and it is. It's not all pretty. Some things are ugly, even. A lot of it hurts. But it's all important, isn't it, even the bad stuff?"

"That sounds very deep."

"I don't know, maybe it isn't, but being down there, you start filling up with the world and the people in it. My brother has a friend. I saw minglers. I want to tell GeeGee all of that. I think she would have understood. Russell, please tell me she's not gone."

"That's quite beautiful, son. But holding on to someone might simply be holding that person back, if you know what I mean. Now, how old was she, this GeeGee? Dark hair? Tall, yes?"

"Not tall, Russell, not tall. She was little. A little

white-faced wrinkled old lady."

He opens the notebook to the placeholder at his finger and flips several pages. He pauses, blinks at the wiry scribbles. "You tell me if this is anything. I wrote 'The boy told the old woman he has just seen a silver lake, and snow—'"

My heart stops dead. "A silver *lake*? Really? I remember silver, I told everybody silver, but I said *lake*? I said *silver lake*? This is so important, Russell."

"It says so right here. I even have the first line of your story."

It snowed at Silver Lake the day I died.

"I didn't get too far, I suppose," he says. "Just one line. But you see? I found inspiration in what you told this person. GeeGee, is it?"

And another piece of the puzzle falls into its place.

"Russell, a guy said I was drowned in a lake. If I told Gee-Gee 'silver lake' when I got here, a silver lake is where I must have died—"

"Oh, for all the love in China!"

The playing cards fly up in the air as that man with pink hair bolts to his feet. "What on earth is that silly woman doing!" He points toward the beach even as he hustles down from the veranda.

I jump up to see an elderly white-haired woman

stumbling down from the foothills. "That's GeeGee! It's her! GeeGee! GeeGee, stop!"

I beat everyone to her. "GeeGee? GeeGee, wait! What are you doing? Did you go through the razor?"

She quivers, turning her face to me. Her face. The skin is translucent, almost clear. Her mouth is slack, her eyes red. "I have to tell them! Tell them . . . tell him . . ."

"GeeGee, who? Me?" I wrap my arms around her shoulders. "I'm here now. I came back."

Pink Hair bustles up. "You sure gave junior a fright, young lady! You all right?"

GeeGee wobbles on her legs, blinking into our eyes for what seems like minutes, before life seeps back to them. "You look alike to me. Which one of you is Denton?"

"It's Denis, GeeGee," I tell her. "You're my great-grandmother."

"Oh? Well, I have something to tell you. It's . . . it's . . . oh, dear . . ."

"Let's get you home," I say. "GeeGee. You can stay at my house."

"That does sound lovely. Do you have tea?"

"Yes. Tea. So much tea!"

Pink Hair pats her hand, then kisses her old cheek, and heads back to the beach club while we work slowly through the neighborhoods to my house. GeeGee is soon chuckling softly to herself. Somehow, like last time, I revive her. She seems a bit bewildered by it all, but once we're settled in my living room, she is happy. The room smells faintly of oranges now, and together we calm down. Telling her what Russell read to me from his book, I remind her what I said when I first came here.

"Maybe you don't remember, but he wrote that I told you *silver lake.*"

Her face goes blank. "Silver Lake does sound familiar. Is it nearby?"

"Maybe. We'll solve this thing after all, thanks to you. Do you remember what you wanted to tell me?"

Her eyelids flicker, as if she's tired. "Something about . . . about . . . oh, I don't know." She looks confused again. "I'll remember, I'm sure. But Silver Lake sounds important. You'd better see to it. Then come home. And watch those stairs. They're very steep!"

34

OCTOBER

Watch those stairs. *They're very steep!*

I still don't know what she means, but I have only myself to blame. It's not just the people down there. I started to forget her, too. Ashamed of myself, I leave her in my house and trudge back to the cold room and hurl myself into the razor. When I push out I steam like a hot carcass.

It couldn't be more than a few minutes after leaving GeeGee in Port Haven before I'm back on the street in front of my house. The sky is gray and frosty over Buckwood. The trees are skeletal. There's a crunch when I move that wasn't here when I left.

It *couldn't* be more than minutes, except it's not minutes. It's not the day I left, or even the same week. Despite the dark I can tell that the leaves are on fire, yellow and red, some layering the ground. The air is clear as glass, chill and biting. It's deep into October, two weeks at least since I left Matt and Dad in Evanton.

"How did this happen?" I whisper to myself. I wrestle to understand, but there's no understanding what I'm doing. No template or game plan. I'm breaking new ground.

Matt will be livid—*is* livid, which I can tell, because his sparks arc down at me from our bedroom like flaming arrows. I feel stupid not to have predicted this. Which he will tell me if he speaks to me at all. But I have to tell him about the lake, maybe the final piece of the puzzle.

I float into his room, ready for his anger, and I'm stunned. It looks like Matt's barely eaten since I left. His clothes are wrinkled and loose. He hasn't cut his hair, and it's dangling in even greasier strands down the sides of his face. The tracers he's shooting off slice and burn me.

I try to be casual. "Hey—"

He throws me an ugly face. "You! You dumbbell! How could you leave me here! You promised to be back for my therapy! It was gross, first alone, then with my parents. So much bawling and groaning. About you, you know! You said you would be back. But no. Liar! Jerk!" He unloads on me for minutes, and I just take it. He's mad, but as furious as his sparks are, there are enough orange ones to tell me he's glad I'm back. Like his good teacher, I nod and wait until he exhausts himself.

"Matt, look, I'm sorry. I have no idea how this happens. Time is weird between the places—"

"*You're* weird!" he snaps. "Dumbo."

"All right, all right. But look, I found something big. It could bust this thing wide open."

"I'd like to bust *you* wide open—"

And I'm thinking how that is exactly what will happen someday, when there's a soft tap on the door.

"What is it?" Matt growls, and I hope it's not Mom because his tone won't make anything better, but it isn't Mom. The door opens a few inches, and Trey's face beams into the room.

"You come here," Matt says, raising his arms weepily, and Trey flies onto the bed, and they huddle like that, a tight single person for minutes.

Trey dries Matt's face, pushes his hair back behind his ears. With one hand, Trey tugs a cellophane-wrapped snack from a pocket—it's a Drake's Cake—teethes it open, and glides it back and forth under Matt's nose, almost comically, to entice him. Matt snortles a sloppy laugh and bites half the thing off. The crumble-top crumbles down his chin, his shirt, onto the bed.

"Ha! Good thing I brought another one." Trey slips out a second cake and, with a kind of flourish, rips it open and bites into it. Crumbs on crumbs.

"Eyebrow is back," Matt says, swallowing and nodding

his chin toward me. "The jerk."

Trey swings around and searches the window. "Denis is here? You can see him right now?"

"Unfortunately. The dope."

"Hey, Denis," Trey says between bites. "Dang, I wish I could see you. You're all he ever talks about. Matt *loves* having you here. I'd be jealous, of course, except you're his brother and you're dead. Seriously, this is so cool."

Sitting on the bed in the rainy light from the window, Trey is so full of life and light, the perfect kind of light. It would be so easy to show myself to Trey, but I know I have to hold off.

"I wish I could talk to Trey," I tell Matt, *"but I think you have to speak for me. Tell Trey it's nice to see Trey, too. Say I'm sorry."*

Matt's listening, half listening, half digging in Trey's pockets for more food, then repeats generally what I said. "He's sorry, the jerkface."

"Don't say that," Trey says softly. "It's really amazing. Your own personal ghost. Or is *ghost*, like, offensive? I don't mean it that way."

"Tell Trey it's all fine. Spirit, soul, ghost, unliving one—"

"*Moron* is another useful term," Matt says, "which he totally is, for being away so long."

Over the next minutes things calm down because of beautiful Trey and the Drake's Cakes, and I realize there's such a complex weave of threads and sparks zinging around and so much life in this room between the two of them that I wonder when any sane person would possibly have *time* to remember someone who has gone on. Sure, you might love that person, or the memory of him or her. But life is so short and shaky, you have to be here for all of it.

Here is what matters. The love, the life, the fabric, the sparks.

And tonight, this little room is the center of the universe.

I move over to my bed and flop down, which Matt has to tell Trey, so Trey doesn't keep staring at the window.

"Here's the thing," I say. *"GeeGee was in a really bad way when I got back, nearly gone, because I started to forget her, too. She has a secret, but can't remember it, probably because I didn't remember her enough. It's mixed up, except I did find out that the first thing I said when I got to Port Haven was, are you ready, 'silver lake.' Silver lake. I know all this because there's a man in Port Haven who writes down stuff, a man called . . ."*

And the name of the white-haired writer escapes me for a second. And a second more. And when I expect it to finally roll off my tongue, it isn't there at all. The longer I wait, the more I can't retrieve it. Electricity shoots across my chest.

"Doesn't matter," Matt says excitedly. "Silver Lake. That sounds so familiar. Like it's a place. That's awesome!"

Trey raises a meek hand in the middle of this. "Sorry, I'm

only getting half the conversation."

It's so strange—and wonderful—to have a second person knowing about me, not judging, not afraid of a dead kid, liking me because of who I was, and being another person I can trust. Trey is a real soul, a good one.

Matt repeats what I told him, while I try to remember the white-haired man's name. I remember his words, though. *It snowed at Silver Lake the day I died. . . .*

"Silver Lake is very good," Trey says, scooping up Matt's laptop, "exceptional, even. There have to be a bunch of Silver Lakes in Pennsylvania, but we'll go to the right one. Well, *you* will." Trey clicks for a few seconds, then grins. "There are three in Pennsylvania, but the detective in me is guessing that since two are near New Jersey, the one we want is the one near . . . Lyndora."

And I'm back in the game. *"Lyndora! Where the Tibbses used to live. That's got to be it!"*

"We have to go there, we have to," Matt says, as if planning a secret mission. He pops up and peeks around the door, listening. "It's so tense around here. Dad is hanging by a thread. I don't know how to get anywhere without kickstarting the apocalypse. Or the end of the world."

Trey snorts a laugh. "Putting aside for a second that the apocalypse *literally* is the end of the world, why not say you want to go for a weekend trip. Say I told you about this cool place. Your mom doesn't even know that a lake is a Denis thing. Neither does your dad, right?"

"Right."

"So tell them you want to forget all this craziness and just hang at this lake, and make it sound like you want to bring the family together. You can't actually say *that*, of course. They'll know something is up. They don't think kids are that smart. But make them think it."

Trey is a little bit of a genius.

"Plus," Trey adds breezily, "you *could* invite *me* on your holiday weekend, and then it would *obviously* be a vacationy thing and all happy-like, because I spread joy wherever I go."

Matt and I look at each other. We grin.

Trey picks up on this and adds a great big smile to ours. "What should I pack?"

35

THE LAKE THAT IS SILVER

Before he breathes so much as a syllable of Trey's plan, Matt chews up nearly a week, worrying the idea over in his brain.

"Are we there yet?" I prod him from my bed.

He turns from his homework. "I have to get Mom at the right time or she'll freeze up. Or worse."

"Worse? What would that look like?"

"She loves you, you know," he says. "Don't be snotty."

When Matt finally sucks it up and asks, it's by floating the idea casually at breakfast before school on Friday. It's touch and go for several very long, gnarly minutes before our parents agree it might actually be all right. Matt smartly throws out that "the therapist *did* say that a change of scene might be good for all of us. There's too much history in our house. Denis, and all."

He flicks his eyes at me with a look of apology, which I accept because I'm so gracious.

As soon as Mom wags her head, as if she's really considering it, Dad's on his phone, swiping away. "Silver Lake in Lyndora, huh? This weekend? If Mommy's okay with it, why not? And why not ask Trey to come with us, yeah?"

Matt's standing over his chair, half frozen, his eyes big. "Really? Are you serious?"

Mom gives a quick nod. And it's done.

"You did it!" I say when we're safely back in Matt's room. I even slap him a high five, as much as a ghost can slap anything. "You got Mom and Dad to drive us to where I was killed. Nice work."

He throws me a face. "When you put it that way . . ."

"No, seriously, this is good. Silver Lake. Silver Lake. It has a kind of pull, doesn't it? 'It snowed at Silver Lake the day I died.' I heard that somewhere. It could be the first line of my story. Aren't you glad I stepped aside and let you work your magic on the parentals?"

He frowns. "The trick will be how to poke around for clues without her suspecting we tricked her. Apocalypse, here we come."

He's right. The more excited Mom gets about his plan to

give the family a break from me, the more she's going to crash when she realizes it's all about me.

We agree to cross that bridge later.

It turns out there is a choice of rooms, and Dad reserves the "Silver Lake Lodge Master Suite Family Weekend Package," a sitting room and bedrooms, one for them, one for Matt, with an extra cot in the sitting room for Trey. An hour after school's out Friday afternoon, Trey's mom rings the kitchen doorbell, and Trey bounces in, beduffeled and ready for fun.

We're in the car before supper. I'm in the back with Matt and Trey, tucked invisibly across the shelf under the back window. Mom and Dad are tenser than you would think, as if they knew what was coming. But then everything is tense since I screwed it all up and got myself killed.

Matt and Trey play that back seat game we used to—I still forget the name and he does too—where you spell words using the first letter of things you see. Like when you spot a car, an airplane, and a tractor—in that order—you can spell C-A-T and get three points. Longer words take more time, but obviously give you more points, and the name of the game itself is the toughest word of all. My recollection is that I usually won, but right now Trey is whupping both our butts.

Trey is smart about Silver Lake, too. Trey recounts what

sounds like one genuine family story after another. "How we saw a bear in the woods" and "I went tubing and the instructor said I held on the longest" and "the morning we found a dead snake on the rug." The beautiful part is that they aren't *exactly* lies because Trey never actually claims these things happened at Silver Lake, which Trey has never been to.

Dad is set to experience all those things. "Except the snake. That I can do without."

It's a pathetically short drive, after all, barely an hour from home to Silver Lake Lodge, a big old wooden structure that might have been built the same year and with the same hoard of logs as the Big Dipper and the Four Pines cabins. It's all railings and porches and peaks of white wood perched on a rise overlooking the lake, which is crystal clear and still, but not as small as any of us believed. I begin to worry that we may not find what we need to here.

"This is big," Mom says. "Great suggestion, Trey. And the woods go on forever. I love the woods. And it's so chilly!" Even as she shivers, she seems to relax. "There are paths all around the lake. I want to hike as soon as we unpack. Kids?"

Matt appears to actually jump. "You bet! Dad?"

"You know, I wish I could," he says mock sadly, "but I have to test out the chairs on the porches." He pauses to wink at Mom, which seems almost odd. "There are three porches and half a dozen chairs on each. I predict it'll take me quite a while."

Odd or not, suddenly there is a spark of light, pale orange, tinged with gold that graces the air. It's not directed at anyone in particular, it just hangs there. Dad's hardly old Dad, and Mom is still a refrigerator, but there is something going on. I think about what they used to be to each other and wonder if they can ever be that again.

Then a sudden cool wind crosses the lake, and I remember why we're here. The mystery of my death could be solved a few hours from now, and I'll slice back to Port Haven to wait out my final, real death. No matter how the idea terrifies me, that's the purpose of all this, right?

To go away?

The air is cold, as clear as glass, and tangy with the smell of evergreens. I scan for the yellow leaves of birch trees, but don't see any. I smell a whiff of woodsmoke pouring from the fireplaces in the lodge, which sends me looking for a looming dark column. There isn't one.

While Mom and Dad run in to register and unpack, Matt, Trey, and I take a short walk down the narrow strip of sand and pebbles that passes for Silver Lake's beach.

Three empty kayaks are pulled up onto the sand. We pause near them, listening to the wind in the treetops. Soon after, a motorboat we can't see crosses the lake, and we watch its ripples wag the kayaks back and forth in the sand.

Matt is the first to say it. "So. Denis. Anything look

familiar? Is this the scene of the crime?"

I drown and float and drown and float.

Trey shivers. "It's horrible to think of a murder being committed in such a beautiful place."

Murder? Yes. Everyone knows that. But again I find that the word pinches me as if it's wrong, or *somehow* it's wrong, in a way I don't know yet. *"Sorry. I got nothing—"*

"Matt, Trey?" Mom calls from the porch. She's wearing short hiking boots, does a happy shuffle on the floorboards. "A quick hike before the sun goes down?"

I don't go with them, but instead glide under a stand of oak trees at the edge of a clearing. Closing my eyes to the beauty of it, I go into myself, think about water, and begin to see . . . a face. Except it's not a face exactly, only a chin, a cheek, an eye. Did I see someone in profile here? If I did, where is the silver? Is it just *silver* because of Silver Lake? But what about the leaves? There are yellow leaves scattered on the ground all over, but they're maple leaves, not birch leaves. The dark presence at the corner of my vision could be a bare tree, I suppose, but the image is so straight in my eye, so clean, not a trunk with branches. I don't know.

I don't.

When the three of them return from the hike, their faces are flushed. The sun has gone. I haven't moved. Matt waves at me to follow, and I do, at a distance. They go into the lodge's dining room. There's another family, a father and two daughters, a mother and a son. They talk like strangers do, comparing notes about summer, towns, schools, holiday plans, whatever. I drift back out. An hour passes, night rolls over the lake. Lamps light the long porches, the boardwalk, the dock. The moon rises. The lake turns silver.

There are miles and miles of forest and hill and lake and nature here, and no light to bleach the dark. Innumerable stars prick the black velvet. The night thickens and clears, heavies and grows lighter than air. Okay, okay. I died here. I died here. I died here?

Matt comes out on the porch and when he calls softly for me, I fade back into the trees.

I don't want to talk. He goes back inside.

Standing at the edge of the forest, I take in the flatness of the lake under the moon, and the lodge lit from inside with all the chatting and laughing—I see Trey and Matt through the windows—and I wonder, what difference does it make how I died?

Maybe I even know the poor soul who did it. What if I pass him each morning at the beach in Port Haven, enjoy the sunshine with him. Or maybe he's worse off than me and has already faded into Garden Hills, forgotten and dead for real.

I should tell Matt to give the whole thing up. Just give it up. At the very least Trey needs the space I'm taking. They all do. I'll go back to GeeGee, hope everyone here forgets me so I can get clean, and climb the hills like I'm supposed to.

Under the unfriendly trees, I resolve to tell Matt in the morning. I'll tell him I'm leaving before we even bother to search for any clues. Forget clues. Forget this.

"And that will be that."

Then the leaves rustle under the tall oaks behind me.

Footsteps crunch among the pine needles.

Turning, I spy a man picking his way among the rocks at the ragged end of the woods. He disappears and reappears, shifting in the blotchy fabric of his jacket. He steps slowly to the water, his moon-cast shadow a black angle on the sand. Then he stops and stares into the lodge's windows, stares at Matt and Trey and my parents, and utters an unspeakable curse.

36

IN COLD WATER

"Matt!" I shout instinctively, not knowing if he'll hear me inside the lodge. *"Matt, get out here!"*

He does hear. He slides quickly and fluidly out the lodge doors onto the porch, careful not to alert the others. Cold has fallen hard. Trey follows closely behind, pausing in the doorframe.

"It's the guy who's been stalking us!" I yell.

Lumbering, but fast, the man heels it for the trees, then falters abruptly, as if he, too, hears my call. A man is taking shape in my mind, not this man. A gangly man, not this man. This man switches back and heads clumsily for the lodge pier.

Trey runs up with Matt, both breathing hard. "The stalker followed us here?"

"*I spotted him outside our house, at school, on the road. There he is!*"

The guy flails on the pier, but the motorboat is chained fast, so he slips into a kayak. He tears the tether loose, but Trey, being such a lake person, slides past Matt, grabs the rope, and swings it around a piling to hold the kayak fast.

I grab onto the man's neck and scream. "*Ssstoppp!*"

The guy gags. "Okay, okay, okay!"

"Who *are* you?" Matt shouts, tugging his phone out and flicking on the flashlight.

The man's face goes blue in the light. I see his balloon of a gut and nearly swallow my tongue. "*It's Sandbag!*"

Matt gapes. "You're Maywell Tibbs!"

"How in heaven you know my name?"

"You killed my brother, you—!" Matt spits out a word I've never heard him use before.

"I didn't!" he says. His beady eyes flicker all around. He knows I'm right there. He can't see me, but he feels me crowding him and he's scared. Breathing a foul breath, he lets his shoulders slump and his hands fall to his lap. "I didn't kill him. Your brother. I knowed it was him, but I didn't kill him. I never meant to, I just wanted money, then I seen the tag on him."

"What tag?" Trey asks.

"His army tag!"

"The dog tag he wore?" Matt says. "You stole it off him, then drowned him here and took him to Gettysburg—"

"Gettysburg! That's clear across the state. I was never there till following you! I got stopped, too. But I didn't have my pickup five years ago. I had Jenny, and Jenny never would have made it there. And this lake? I never been here before."

"Liar!" Matt spits. "And stop talking like a bad movie. We know you grew up in Lyndora. Melrose said you drowned a dog in a lake. This lake!"

Something in Maywell Tibbs cracks. He pauses but can't quite lose his way of speaking. "I never drowned no dog. Any dog. If I told Melrose I did, it was to scare him. I never been here and I never stole your daddy's dog tag. He is a vet. I seen his tag on your brother." His eyes flicker in the light of a lazy spray of white sparks. "Stronger than money is brothers in the service. You don't steal tags."

"You've been stalking them," Trey snaps. "We all know it. Why?"

Maywell thrusts a finger at Matt. "Since I seen *you* in the band at St. Francis hospice weeks back. My momma, Momma-May, is dying there. I nearly died, too, seeing your face. I thought you would sic the cops on me for taking your brother, until I recollect you never saw me. But I followed you. Then you went to that coaster so I thought you knew."

Matt's hands shake. "What were you going to do, kill me, too?"

"How? If the daddy of your twin is a vet, so is *your* daddy a vet. Plus, I tode you, I didn't kill your brother, I let him go the next morning."

"Tuesday? Are we talking about Tuesday? And stop the dumb talk!"

"Ask him where. If he didn't kill me, where did he take me?"

Matt does, and after a few breaths, Maywell says, "Who do *you* talk to when you need answers? I asked Daddy what to do, and he give me his answer. And what you think he said? 'Let him go,' he said. It started to snow right then. But I did. I let him go. . . ."

It started to snow right then.

It started to snow.

Snow.

And like a rush of frigid air, I see flakes drifting against the gray dark sky, then more flakes among bare trees, falling and falling, and the yellow leaves becoming white on the ground. The dark shape at the edge of my eye is there. The man in camouflage is there. Not this man. Another man. I am suddenly exhausted, sullen.

"He's telling the truth," I say. *"White sparks means he's telling—"*

"Matt! Trey!" It's Dad, shouting from the lodge porch. "Where are you two?"

Maywell uses the distraction. He pushes Matt away and jumps out of the kayak. Even with his gut, bigger than I remember it, he's up the bank and into the woods in a flash.

Matt jumps after him. "Stop him! He kidnapped and tortured you!"

"Matt!" Dad yells.

"*Forget him,*" I say. "*When this is over, tell Dad to call the detective, Sparn. Maywell will pay for what he did. But he didn't kill me. We don't need him right now.*"

"Are you guys all right?" Dad huffs, running toward us.

"Yeah," says Trey. "Just poking around. Enjoying the night."

I hear a truck start up. It drives off. The sound of the engine fades, and it's just us and the stillness settling over the lake.

The quiet doesn't last. The door bangs behind us as Mom storms out of the lodge, holding a folder in her hands. I know instantly what it is, Matt does too. His police file.

"You tricked me!" she shouts, brushing past Trey, who stands openmouthed, staring at Matt. "You two tricked me—again."

"Tricked you? How?" Dad is puzzled. "Bonnie, calm down. What are you talking about?"

"The police file," Mom says, shaking it at him. "I found it in Matt's things. This is all about Denis, I know it. That's the *only* reason we're at this lake. You're searching and digging for clues about Denis. You cooked this up together. And I fell for it!"

"Bonnie, I don't know what this is about, but for me it's just a weekend. Like Matt said. It's beautiful here."

"Mom—" Matt starts, but she continues in a very quiet voice that is hard as iron.

"I don't know if I can stay, Gary."

"Where? Here?"

"With you!" she said. "I don't think I can. I've already called a car to pick me up. I'm going home. You keep doing this, and it's killing us. More than that, you can't drag Matt through this hell."

Matt inches toward Trey, pleading with his eyes. "Mom, you have this all wrong—"

Dad puts his hand up to Matt. In the silver glow of the moon, he gives Mom an almost casual expression, a look as still as hers is angry. "You know, as far as I know, this has nothing at all to do with Denis, but you think I'm dragging Matt through hell? Well, it's where we live now."

"No, Gary. It's where *you* live. You've lived there for five years. Heck, since your father first hit you, you've been in hell. The rest of us don't have to live there. The rest of us can leave the past in the past. You could leave all that behind, too. You *could*, but you don't want to. You love it, the death and blood, the leg, the girl, all of it . . ."

The girl? What girl?

To Dad, the hugeness of how she's wrong is too big to fight, to answer in any way he knows, especially not on the lakeshore, with Trey right there. All three of us know that Dad is clueless about Silver Lake, but he just takes it, not knowing what words to come out with. Mom thinks his silence means he *expects* her to leave. It doesn't mean that at all. But Mom thinks it does.

She breathes for almost a minute in the silence of the night, trembling from head to toe.

"This is it. I can't take it anymore. I wake up each morning already crushed by the day ahead, and here we are on a sick chase after something that isn't there. The police are done with it. I'm done with it. Only you aren't. Denis is gone. Gone, gone."

She throws the police file down, its contents sliding out on the ground, the photos catching the moonlight. Faltering back to the lodge, she manages to enter and disappear without a sound.

Matt watches her, then turns. "Dad, I'm sorry. I'm really sorry. This is all my fault—"

Dad stands there out of breath. "No, it's not. It's not." He's black in the moon shadows. Trey hovers nearby, waiting for something to happen without knowing what that might be. I shouldn't be sensing anything as strongly as I am now, and I know it's reckless, but there's a heaviness growing in me, weighing me. I'm doing something no one I know has done, staying here so long, going so deep, clinging so close to my twin brother, that I'm . . . I don't even know what the word is.

"Should we go to her?" Matt whispers. "Say it's my fault, and that I'm so sorry?"

"Not yet." Dad rocks like he did at the battlefield, stinging with the revelation that Mom wakes *already crushed by the day ahead.* "Let her cool down. I need to talk with you. Trey, sorry . . ."

"I'll see you inside," Trey replies, then runs to gather up the contents of the file.

Dad works his way to the shoreline, Matt by his side. As much as I don't want to, I follow them. The idea of secrets makes me sick. What will Dad say? Could there possibly be any more pain still hidden?

They wander along the beach. I wait, Matt waits quietly. Dad says nothing. In their minds they run over Mom's outburst, which wasn't even an outburst, but seemed deadly logical.

Because, of course, she's right. This has to end. Dad and Matt have to give up scratching and scraping and digging for answers, because the noise is killing our family. A solution has to be found—or not found—but my life has really got to end.

Dad finally stops by the water, a half mile from the lodge. His look is faraway. I can't tell whether he's about to shut down or get mystical. When he speaks, it's as if to himself.

"I didn't tell you everything that happened the day my father died."

Matt tenses, like at Gettysburg. He knows something bad is coming.

"You probably heard Mom say there was a girl, right? There was. On the bus. Third grade. She died in the crash, too. Thrown. A window shattered, and, well, whatever. She died."

Matt's knees nearly buckle. "Dad . . ."

"It was one holy mess that day, and the real reason I served time after I left the hospital. The parents sued everyone. My father's estate, which was a joke, there was nothing, the junky house. Then they somehow proved the bus driver had had blackouts, so they sued the city. They were destroyed. Gabby's parents. That was her name. Gabby Tornillo."

Matt eyes me, then looks down. His feet are planted in the sand, his face is drained of color. "Dad, I'm so sorry." It strikes me that Matt is hearing things kids aren't usually told. Dad so badly needs to have someone to tell, someone who loves him and says so.

"That time, that whole thing, was the worst in my life. That's why . . ." Dad jams his eyes shut, squeezing tears down his cheeks, which he quickly wipes. "You know that's why . . ."

"Matt, bring him back. Don't push it. He's remembering horrible stuff."

But it's not over for Matt. "Dad? That's why what?"

"Don't you get it? That's why Denis was taken from us. Taken from you. Because of the girl. Because of what I did. The horrible thing I did—"

"Dad! No! No. That doesn't make sense! Dad, no."

At exactly that moment, I hear a frantic whisper from the suite inside the lodge. It's Mom. She calls in a way I haven't heard in so long.

"Denis . . . Denis . . ."

Wrenching myself away from my brother and father on the shore, I fly back to the lodge. *"Mom?"*

I find her in the room, leaning over the edge of the bed like a slumped S. On the floor next to her is her bag, packed and bulging. She's staring into space.

"Mom. Matt and Dad are on their way back. Mommy, I love you, don't leave."

She checks the time on her phone, throws it in her bag.

"Mom, stay. Please stay. Matt needs you. I'll go away the instant we finish this, I promise. They'll be back in a few minutes. Mommy, stay!" I stand in the moonlight from the window. There should be enough light to see me if she wants to. *"Mom, I'm here, I'm right here. Mom, it's Denis. Mom!"*

All of a sudden a scent of oranges overpowers me. I whirl around, and there is GeeGee, teetering in the corner, her face a mask of white, with a thin red line down the center. Her eyes are black and slightly offset. They glint in the light. Her mouth twists painfully.

"Tell them!" she cries thickly. *"He was there! Tell them!"*

"GeeGee? You can't be here!" I step to her, but she jerks toward my mother.

"Someone please tell them. I can't help anymore. But someone must!"

"You can't be here! It's too dangerous!"

She turns to me, and a look of horror flashes in her eyes. Her chest convulses, she staggers back. I go to embrace her, when she thrusts her hands to her face and shrieks at the top of her lungs. The cries of Melrose Tibbs rush back to me, and I wrap her heaving shoulders in my arms.

"GeeGee, stop! Stop this! I'm taking you back! Don't do this. I love you. I remember you!"

And her wail loses its breath in a ragged cry. Her quaking limbs calm under my touch. She releases her hands from her face, and though she is crying, sobbing, the line of red down her face whitens, her cheeks draw subtle color into them, she turns her eyes up to me.

"De . . . Denis . . . ?"

"I'm taking you home now. Come with me."

"Yes. Yes. Yes."

Still holding my great-grandmother tightly in my arms, I turn to my mother.

"Stay, just a few minutes more, Mom, please!"

I shout these words as I reach one hand to her, hoping she'll feel even the barest touch. But she puts her fingers right through where I am and lifts the window shade. A car with its lights on is in the parking lot, waiting for her. She picks up her bag.

"*Tell them!*" GeeGee cries to her. But it's too late.

"Good-bye," Mom whispers to the empty room that isn't empty at all. She walks out the door, and the room collapses into dead space.

Not five minutes after the car peels away, Matt runs in the room. "Mom?"

"*She left,*" I say. "*She didn't want to go. But she couldn't wait. Sorry, I have to take GeeGee home.*"

"No. No!" He searches for Mom's luggage, then falls to his knees.

I leave with GeeGee just as Dad hurries into the room. The loneliness of it hits him squarely in the face. My last view of him is as he sits on the bed where she just sat and cries into his hands.

37

IRON NOVEMBER

Like Macy Tibbs took his son Melrose back to Port Haven, I push through the razor with GeeGee. I'm sliced more painfully than ever, terrified I'm leaving something vital behind, but I can't look, can't think about it. GeeGee might have been cut far more deeply than I am, the result of too many times visiting there, but my cut takes the brunt of it.

"You poor boy!" she exclaims when we hit the streets. "But I think we made it in one piece!"

"I'll check later. GeeGee, tell me what you wanted to tell my mom. You said 'tell them' and 'he was there.' Tell who? And who was where?"

She looks me square in the face, reaches up to smooth my

left eyebrow with her shaking fingers. "That's the point. He was at my house!"

"Who, GeeGee? My dad? My dad lived with you, I know that. What about it?"

She shakes her head. "No, no, not him. Not that house. The other house. In Kittanning."

The contents of the suitcase shudder back to me. The photo of an old house with a porch.

"The farmhouse? Are you talking about the white farmhouse? That was your house! We were there, Matt and I, weren't we? But my dad doesn't know that, does he? He doesn't know we were ever there, does he?"

GeeGee shakes her head. "Oh, no. We weren't speaking by then. But that's where it all happened. She can tell you. It was terrible, but she can tell you."

"She? My mother?"

"He was wrong, he was sorry. After it happened. He changed."

"Who was sorry? Who changed?"

"We're all doing our poor human best, aren't we? I think we are. I hope we are, I do."

It strikes me right then that, out of the entire living world, only my mother knows what happened at the farmhouse. *We're all doing our poor human best?*

"Stay here, GeeGee. I'll be back!"

• • •

Long story short, I hurl myself into the razor. What is this, my tenth time? It's bloody. Enough said. Back in Buckwood, I can tell by the light that it should be afternoon, and Matt will be at school, but something's wrong. The sun is low in the sky, flat behind the trees. And there is wind, a cold wash of air down the street, but the sound of the wind is not in the trees because the trees are bare. It is the rustle of curled brown leaves leaping and spinning on the ground.

And I know in my gut it's November.

The minutes I was in Port Haven have betrayed me again, worse this time. It could be as long as a month since I left Matt at Silver Lake. It is the month of my death.

As quickly as I can, I wing it to school and fly through the halls, already feeling the sparks of anxiety and anger flying off Matt. I see Trey first and brush Trey's shoulder briefly, which stops Trey dead in the hall, looking all around and finally up at me.

Trey gasps a sob, laughs brightly, then points back up the hall to the corner.

"Chem lab!"

I give a nod, which Trey pretends to catch as a kiss on the cheek. I slither fleetly toward the lab, when all of a sudden I am broadsided by a single barbed shard of black fire.

It's coming from my house.

Putting Matt on hold, I soar back home to find Mom and Dad quivering on the doorstep. Dad holds an overnight bag. Mom is in her business suit. She is crying, weaving back and forth.

"Gary, please not now. Not again, but certainly not now."

He shakes his head. "It's time. I have to go. I'll be back."

I step in front of Dad, try to catch the light. *"Dad, where are you going? Why? Why now?"*

"You can't go, not with Matt this way," she says. "The therapist said he needs us together. He's been in a dark place for weeks now. You're part of it. It's important—"

"This is important too, Bonnie."

"For who, Gary? For you? For her?" Mom slashes the tears away from her cheeks with the backs of her hands, and they fly as jagged sparks at Dad, sending him down a step. "Gary, you know how you get. It'll be worse this time."

"A couple of days. That's all."

"Really, you're going to abandon us. Just like you always do. You know what happens, don't you? Five years ago. Do I have to remind you? You're going to drink and drink—"

He throws his bag to the driveway. "I'm not going to drink! We've been over this—" He cuts himself off and balls his fists into his pockets to trap them there.

"You're going to leave us, knowing there's someone out there? You've seen him."

Dad heaves in a breath. "Bonnie . . ."

"Then you know what, Gary? Go! Just go!" She waves her hand at the car, scoops up her pocketbook, and is inside in an instant, slamming and latching the door behind her.

Dad stares at, then softly pushes, the door, in no way hard enough to open it, even if it weren't locked. A cold breeze comes down the driveway from the side yard. He turns, walks around the car, picking up his duffel on the way. He gets in. The engine roars. He goes.

I slip in the door to find Mom sitting on the floor at the foot of the stairs, sobbing. I have no idea what I just saw. Short fierce bolts of light burst on the floor around her.

"Mom, I'm sorry I left you. I'm sorry I died and messed it up even more."

Ten minutes later, not even, Matt runs in the front door, yelling, "Dad!" When he sees me hovering, he is boiling mad and ready to scream. Then Mom appears like an apparition at the top of the stairs in a bathrobe.

Matt is stunned by her face, a white mask of tears. "Mom . . . ?"

From the shadow of the landing, she clumsily tells him the bare details. "Your father is gone. He'll be back in a few days. Don't ask me anything. I'll make supper later. I'm going to bed."

She pivots on her bare heel and goes into her room, closing the door quietly behind her.

He stares up at the landing, then wheels around angrily to me. "You idiot! You jerk! Where *were* you?" He punches the air where my chest is, and it hurts more than I can say. Jerking his phone from his pocket, he hits the screen and sobs at it. "Come here *now!*" Then he pushes past me and jumps double steps up the stairs.

"Where is Dad going?" I ask when we get to his room.

He flashes a pair of dark eyes at me. "How should I know? The only thing I *do* know is that we can't find your killer until Dad gets back from wherever he went because Mom's certainly not going to take me anywhere!"

I sit on my bed and roll that over in my mind. "I'm not sure we have to wait."

"Oh, let me trust you. Watch." He burns a look right at me, not needing any trick of the light now. "I should have expected this. Dad's been dark since we got back from Silver Lake. They patched it up, sort of, when we got back, but day by day, it's been getting worse. He couldn't sit down, always pacing. He shouted at Mom the other day. They both shouted. But what do you care? Gone for a month while I'm dying here! Some brother."

"Okay, okay. How many times can I say it? I'm sorry. But look, something weird happened at GeeGee's house in Kittanning. It was her house Mom brought us to when we were two."

He looks up at me, goes through a bunch of words in his head before he says, "Why?"

"I'm not sure. GeeGee's confused and says 'he was there.'

I don't now who 'he' is, and apparently Dad doesn't know, but Mom does. We need to unravel the threads—"

"You and your idiotic threads. You ask Mom. Go ahead. See how far you get!"

"Matt, look—"

Trey bursts in almost on cue, pushing right past me.

"He's here again," Matt snarls, with an unkind finger gesture at me.

Trey looks around for me. "I knew it. I felt it. I have feelings about things."

"The dope is all about me asking Mom what happened at GeeGee's house in Kittanning ten years ago. Oh, and my dad just bolted. Again. So Mom's a wreck. Again."

Trey makes a face. "Yeah, that's a tough one, Denis. She gets in these moods and goes zombie."

"The instant she realizes it's a *you* thing, she'll die," Matt says. "Plus, she'll never talk. Ever. Ever. Ever."

"*Unless you give her something,*" I tell him.

Matt looks at me. "Give her something?"

"Like what?" Trey asks.

"*Move my bed out of your room.*"

"What? No. Your bed stays here."

"*Move it out, and she'll think you're really over me.*"

"I *am* over you. I'm so over—"

"*You're not, and she knows it.*"

"But I want your bed in here. Where are you going to

hang out when you come? Where are you going to sit?"

"On your head."

What I don't tell him is that I'll be leaving soon anyway, that I have to leave soon or I'll be so messed up for the rest of my death. I don't tell him, but I will have to. He's my brother, and when you have to leave, you say good-bye properly to your brother. I didn't get to the last time.

"Don't tell her. Just take the bed apart and move it out. Then say to her, oh, by the way, Mom, about that old lady's house. . . ."

38

THE PLACE I USED TO BE

After Trey lovably approves the plan, it happens exactly that way.

Not that night, of course, or the next night, or even the next, because Matt has to stall until he can't possibly stall anymore. He waits until Trey can make it back for dinner one night. At the table he offhandedly asks Trey to help him afterward.

"Help? Doing what?" Mom says as she and Trey wash blueberries and pick off their stems before dropping them on ice cream.

"Muscle," Trey says, flexing both arms comically. They're pretty soft.

Mom laughs. "Okay, then."

That night after Trey leaves, Mom taps on Matt's bedroom door, the room that used to be ours. I watch her kiss him good night but linger on the edge of the bed. I remember how she used to go from one pillow to the other, alternating night after night for who to kiss first. I sense how it still grieves her to have only one son now.

"Good night, sweetie. Another day done. See you in the morning." She swivels toward the other bed on her way out. "Oh!"

"Yeah. Trey helped me. It's in the attic. But it's okay. Denis is . . ."

"*Right here!*"

". . . gone. Like you said."

"Matt, I'm so sorry. I didn't ask . . . I didn't even hear you two."

"Stealth. Trey and I are perfecting it. But it was time, you know? Maybe because Dad's not here or something. I don't know. It just seems right."

By giving this to her, little by little, Matt proves he's one of the cleverest people I know.

She lowers and kisses her forehead to his. "I love you."

"Mom?"

"Yes?" Her voice is so soft.

"When will Dad be back? Days? Longer? He'll come back before . . . you know, won't he?"

"Of course, but Matt . . ." She draws in a long breath,

opens her lips to speak, then closes them into a flat smile. Another breath, and she starts, "Honey, you see what's happening. I know you do. No matter how hard he tries, Daddy can't get away from his dark thoughts. He's chained to them like some poor old dog."

"He said Denis died because of what happened to the girl. I told him no, but . . ."

"He told you about her, then?" She stiffens. "Well, it's her, Denis, his own father. He feels responsible for all of it. It falls on him like a huge weight this time of year. This horrible month. This year is especially bad. The girl would have been twenty-one this month. Denis would be twelve, like you, but isn't. It's just a horrible time."

"Is she the one you and Dad were arguing about?" he asks.

Mom nods. "He's gone to visit her. Her grave. In Valdosta. He drove there five years ago, too, the week before we went to that terrible amusement park. His 'business trip.' You remember that, right?"

Right. The day we went to Funland, Dad was extra lively. So. He'd just come back from the mess in Valdosta. Maybe he felt he needed a break from the pain of it. Then I happened.

"Matt, I've tried," Mom goes on. "I keep trying. I'm chained too, right? Your father and I are tied together forever, I guess. But day after day? He's digging at the ground about Denis, this year is really bad, and he roped you into it.

We can't let it happen to *us*, Matt, not like to him."

Matt wants to scream, protest, throw something. He wants to tell her it's him too, and not just Dad. He wants her to know I'm right here with her and that *I'm* involved too. But he also knows the past weeks have been leading exactly here. And that she's right.

"I guess. I get it. But . . . there's one last question I have. Please don't get mad. It's just a tiny thing, then it's over. Really over. I promise. Cross my heart and . . ."

She closes her eyes for a second, opens them, and glances at where my bed used to be. "Matt . . . all right. Make it quick, though, please. Okay?"

He breathes in, out. "So, it's our great-grandmother's house."

"Her house?"

"I saw a picture of it. The farmhouse. I remember it now."

"You remember it?"

"The porch, the big windows. I was small. Around two, right? Denis was there too. Dad doesn't know. But you brought us to her house. We had vaccinations there. But that's not everything, is it? Mom, please tell me. The last thing, and it's over."

Over. The word kills me.

Mom sits up, then lowers her head so we can't see her face. "It was ten years ago. Daddy took off for the first time, I didn't know he was going to the girl's grave. He just left. I had to find him. I took you boys to his grandmother's house. She was living in Kittanning then. You were small. I wanted to ask her if she knew where he'd gone. I didn't know anyone I could trust. I carried Denis up those steep front steps. He was asleep. It was late. I held your hand and you climbed up by yourself, so brave, not knowing why, but just being a good little boy."

As Mom speaks, the fog of time thins away, and the farmhouse begins to rise around me like a dream made real.

39

I FELL ASLEEP

The old house builds itself, board by board, from the cold gray yard. It is ten years ago.

I enter. The front room is small and square and close. Pale light seeps from the room on the left, where a dark painting of Jesus in the Garden, weeping blood, hangs over the buffet. Ahead, a narrow set of black stairs leads up.

"She lived only a few years in the Kittanning house," Mom says. "As far as I know, your father never visited her. She blamed him for what happened to her son, *his* father. She took it back, finally, but it didn't make any difference to him. He broke with her, but she was always kind to me. And to you."

Matt turns to me. "I never knew. You must have been so afraid for us. For Dad, too."

A tiny voice fluttered down the stairs. Feet tramped down a hall, two sets, one lightly, on tiptoe, the other clacking heavily. Beyond the top step was a small room with a wooden crib wedged against a wall. A child moaned softly inside.

The child was me.

"Matthew, please! You're wearing me out!" GeeGee said ten years ago.

The phone began to ring. And ring and ring. GeeGee chased Matt, who ran like a crazy child. "Matt, stop!"

"It was that—this—horrible month," Mom says. "I found out later that it was the little girl's birthday, as it would be every year around now. I didn't know that then. I was terrified when he left, didn't know what to do, so I took you to his grandmother's and went off to find him. Talk about chained. I loved him, love him, and I was afraid of what he might do. I drove everywhere, called everyone I knew. I searched for days. Then your great-grandmother phoned me—"

"I call her GeeGee," Matt says.

She looks quizzically at him. "Okay. GeeGee phoned me that she'd gotten you your vaccinations, but now Denis had a fever. I was going to come right to you, when it finally hit me what the date was and that he might have gone to Georgia. His terrible place. So I called her back to say I needed a couple more days. But this time she—GeeGee—didn't answer the phone. I kept calling. Still no answer. I got in my car and drove straight to you."

My head was splitting, burning. The gray house closed in, suffocating me. I rocked in the crib, back and forth, my face on fire, while Matt ran like a maniac. The phone stopped ringing.

GeeGee came to me. She leaned over the railing and put a cool palm on my forehead. "Do you feel better yet?"

Matt galloped in, roaring, "Me! Me! Memememe!"

"Please, stop," she cried. The phone started again. She took her hand away. I wailed.

"What did you find when you got there?" Matt whispers this.

From her sparks I know that Mom's remembering driving. "What do you remember?"

Matt is at the house now too. "The phone rang and rang. Denis cried, but I couldn't stop bouncing. I saw GeeGee lie down on her bed, but not answer the phone. It kept ringing."

Mom is trying to read Matt's face. "Anything else?"

"There was pounding on the front door. That was you?"

"I had a key," she says.

"You pounded anyway. The phone and the doorbell were both ringing. But she was already sleeping. 'Phone!' I told her. 'Phone!' And you kept pounding on the door."

Mom looks out the black window. "No, Matt. I was the one calling. It wasn't me at the door."

All the noise! I stood in my crib. My legs stiffened. I saw Gee-Gee across the hall on her bed, I cried for her, but the hall between the rooms suddenly darkened with a shape.

"Daddy?" I said, and reached for him, but my legs collapsed. I fell over the crib rail to the floor. My eye was wet and hot and my eyebrow burned. I howled. The shape came at me.

"When I drove into the driveway," Mom whispers, "the house was dark, the front door was wide open. I heard Denis screaming his head off, but the moment I ran in, he stopped. He stopped crying, like someone threw a switch. I ran up the stairs, terrified. I shouted for her, but she didn't answer. Gee-Gee didn't answer. I ran into Denis's room and I saw him. Him."

I felt his arms around me. I was lifted, I floated up.

"Who? Mom, who was it?"

"He held Denis in his arms and rocked him back and forth. Like Daddy used to."

I stopped my crying. I floated up.

"Who was it?"

"A man, some man! I screamed at him. He didn't move. He just rocked Denis and stared at a photograph of a Civil War soldier. I ran at him, screaming, but he just set Denis down in his crib and pushed past me. It was some horrible stranger. I remember he smelled like oil or ashes or something foul. He'd broken into the house. He'd picked up Denis, then he just . . . ran away."

Matt's mouth hangs open. My heart is pounding. But we both remember now. It's seared in memory, and we both know this moment.

"What happened then?" he finally says. "Where was I?"

"I scooped Denis in my arms. Then I saw blood on his eyebrow. And on the floor. He must have fallen from his crib. I called for you. You were in your great-grandmother's room, hopping around her bed like a bunny." Mom chokes on a sob, reaches for him.

"I was trying to wake her up," he says. "She was sleeping. I needed to wake her up."

"But you couldn't." Mom leans over and hugs him. "I'm so sorry, Matt. She had gone."

"Gone?" He goes frigid. "She was . . . She *died* while we were there? I made GeeGee chase me around? While Denis was crying? And the phone rang and rang? Seriously? I killed her!"

"Matt, no. Never!" Mom is sobbing outright now, holding him. "You were two! She was eighty. It was my fault for leaving two babies with an old woman. It was her heart—"

I stagger back to where my bed used to be. *You wear me out! Are you feeling better? I fell asleep!* GeeGee's words rush at me.

The threads. The threads! Where do they start, where do they end?

GeeGee died because because because . . .

Matt wipes his face. "Who was the intruder? Did you ever find him?"

"No, no. He'd vanished. I put you in the car and drove home as quickly as I could. I called the Valdosta police to get a message to your father. Daddy came back. The man, whoever he was, never returned."

"Did he wear camouflage? Ask her that."

"I . . ." Matt searches for me, sees me, pleads with me, but seems unable to ask the question.

"Never mind. I know he did."

Mom sits up a little, tries to regain whatever she can of herself. She manages to breathe. "That's all I know. The terrible secret. Your great-grandmother died while I was trying to find your dad, and you were alone with some stranger. Only for minutes, but yes, there it is."

"Dad doesn't know about the man?"

"I didn't tell him the circumstances, no. The first time I told him something like that, two people died. I never reported it, either, because the man ran away, and Denis was all right."

"But you never told Dad?"

"Don't you get it, Matt? Your GeeGee died because I abandoned you there! Or maybe because Daddy abandoned us. We were so shaky then, him and me, it was just easier not to tell him. Or you. Or anyone. It was just easier." She wipes her cheeks and sits upright on the edge of the bed.

"So, this ends it, Matt, yes?"

He tries to bring it all together in a way that, right now, seems completely impossible. So of course he can't bring it together. He fails to tie it off. It bleeds like severed arteries.

He says the opposite.

"That ends it, Mom. Thanks."

"All right, then," she says. "Time to sleep."

She steps back, hugs him for a second, then again for a long time. Gazing at where my bed used to be, she walks to the door. I blow my nonbreath on her face. A couple of strands of hair move. I can't be sure she even feels it. She switches off the lamp and pulls the door closed against the downstairs lights.

40

MISSING SOMEONE

We're both roaring inside, our hearts slamming against our ribs.

"That's it," Matt hisses. "The big secret. We—you and me, but mostly me—killed GeeGee."

"No, you didn't."

"Oh, yes, I did." He pounds his mattress with both fists. "And we're still nowhere! That's the worst part. Who killed you? We don't know. What did GeeGee mean? Ten years ago there was a stranger? A creep who broke into her house that no one ever found? Fine, but why Gettysburg, why give clues to your murder? Maybe Maywell Tibbs lied, after all!"

This doesn't sit right. "Except I believe him. I believe that Maywell let me go."

"Well, that makes one of you. But if *he* didn't kill you, who did? Riddle me that."

Thousands of thoughts race in my head and none of them answer that question.

"Who did?" he repeats. "For Gettysburg to make *any* sense at all, the killer has to have a connection to Georgia. But there isn't one. This stranger person is no one, not even a clue. Maybe Dad was right. It's random. We have nothing. Nothing!"

"No," I whisper, almost to myself. "We're missing someone. There's more—"

He snorts sharply. "Yeah, or guess what, maybe there *isn't* more, and there's no solving this because it can't be solved, and this—*this*—is the way it is. Mom and Dad won't be getting back together, and all I have is just year after year of horrible Novembers forever."

The room looks strangely empty without my bed, not that I need it. This isn't my home.

"First thing in the morning I'll call Dad about Maywell Tibbs. He asks his father what to do, and his father says 'let you go'? That's just creepy-guy lingo for '*murder* him,' I'm sure of it."

His phone vibrates. He slides it out of the covers and holds it up. "Trey."

"Answer it."

"It's late. I'm shaking. I don't want to."

"Answer it," I say.

He gives me a face, swipes it open, hits speaker. "Denis can hear you—"

"We need to talk," Trey says in a whisper. "I broke it open. The case. The thing you—well, all of us—have been looking for."

"It's not open. It's closed. I just had a big thing with Mom. It's over, Trey. Good night."

"It's not over. Not yet. Denis, tell your dumb brother I just found something beyond big. It's huge. H-U-G-E. You'll have to travel, but you'll just need your bike, some cash, and Denis."

Matt snorts. "And I don't really need him—"

"Meet me before school tomorrow, early. I'll show you everything."

Trey hangs up. Matt stares at the phone, says nothing. Neither do I. After the last living-room light flicks off, there's the sound of feet on stairs and then the master bathroom faucet. A few minutes later Mom's bedroom door closes. After that it's dark and quiet in the house.

Matt lies awake. "I trust Trey, but if this goes nowhere, the whole thing is over, and I'm done. I am so done!"

"Me too."

But I'm trembling like a leaf. It has to be over, I know that. But then what?

• • •

In the morning he silently pulls on his clothes. We've already said all there is to say to each other. It's bitter cold, bleak and pitch-black out. He wears two T-shirts, two actual shirts, and a thick sweater. Breakfast is as normal as it can be.

"It's freezing out there," Mom says. "I'll drive you."

He swallows his juice. "No, thanks. I want to bike. It might be the last time for a while. And there's a test first period, so I'm meeting Trey early to study. But I'll call you."

They hug. "I love you," she says.

"Love you, Mom."

And it's true, he does love her. The angry way he bangs out the door proves it. He jumps past the garden to the shed and practically tears the latch off. After wheeling out his bike, he redoes the latch, and wheels the bike down the driveway to the street.

It's early, all right. Not a soul around except me.

I find myself instinctively checking for gray pickups, but I know Maywell Tibbs's part in this is truly over, even if Matt isn't sure. The man I see in my mind is not him. The man hurtling among the yellow leaves in the falling snow is someone else.

Matt looks blankly at me, then at the house. It's so dark and cold.

"You okay?" I ask as he pedals silently to the corner.

"What do you think? I hate lying to Mom. I hate all of this."

"I get it. Last time, bro. I'm pretty sure."

I'm also pretty sure "last time" means something different to both of us.

Too few minutes later we're rolling into the school parking lot. My mind is a whirling jumble of faces and places. Trey is sitting on the curb, laptop out. Only the custodians and kitchen staff are inside. I can tell from their cars.

"He's here." Matt thumbs toward me, giving Trey a quick embrace.

"Hey, Denis. No time for ghost hugs, even if we could," Trey says, brushing the sweaty hair from Matt's forehead. "This is it. It's about Macy Tibbs, the father you saw at the Lincoln Inn encampment. Take a look."

Trey flips up the laptop. The screen flashes to life. It's Melrose Tibbs's obituary in the *Butler Eagle*, appearing the Saturday after I died. It's the same one he had me read to him.

"We know this, Trey," Matt says. "Denis read it out at the hotel."

"Apparently not well enough. Listen to it again."

Trey focuses on the screen. "'He is survived by his mother, Maybelline, currently of Buckwood, but predeceased by his father, Macy Tibbs, a decorated veteran of the Korean War, formerly of Coraopolis.'"

Matt shoots me a look. "I know that. We read those same words. Trey—"

"Define *read*. Come on, Matt! *Predeceased by his father*. If *Macy* Tibbs died *before* his son Melrose—who died *the same day* as Denis—how could his other son *Maywell* possibly ask his father what to do with the kid in his trunk? Answer me that!"

Matt narrows his eyes. "All it means is that Maywell lied to us—"

"Unless he didn't," Trey says, with an inch of a smile. "There's only one place you go to talk to someone who's dead, right?"

"Trey, seriously. It's freezing—"

"The cemetery! Maywell asked his father's advice at his tombstone. Which means we know exactly where he dropped Denis off on the day he died. Done! And done!"

Matt squints at Trey for what seems like minutes, his face going through a bunch of expressions before he grabs Trey's shoulders and shakes.

"That's brilliant! Trey, you are brilliant!"

"I know it. I've known it for a while, but I— What the— Whoa!"

I've rushed into Trey's arms, which Trey doesn't exactly *feel*, but *knows*, because Trey nearly falls to the sidewalk. "I felt that! Denis, I felt that! Wow. But you know the very best part? The cemetery is only a bus ride away."

"Where?" I ask, and it's suddenly as if Trey can hear me, too.

"St. Timothy's churchyard," Trey says. "In Zelienople."

Matt shoots me a look. "Zelienople. Where Dad lived with GeeGee!"

And I see the camouflaged man move stealthily across my mind. I press at the figure, claw at this raw fragment of memory, but he vanishes among the white birch trees.

Zelienople, a town thirty-eight miles from Funland, twenty-four miles from Buckwood.

Zelienople, the place where I died.

I turn to Matt. *"This is it. The thread that connects the kidnappers to our family. Zelienople where the threads cross. It's where we'll understand the last few hours of my life."*

"And discover the identity of your killer."

Watching his face, I sense that every tick of Matt's brain toward the solution is one tick closer to me fading into the hills, away from all this. Is he torn? Does he want it to end?

He gives me his answer too soon.

"We're going there now."

"It's right on the bus line," Trey says, bringing up a map on the computer. "You can bike to the station. I'll cover for you. I know my parents will, too, if I have to loop them in."

I imagine Matt and Trey together, and know that they're already closer than we ever were. It's obvious that Matt's got a fine future without me. He can do anything in the world.

A final hug, a shiver in the cold, and we're on our way.

41

A TOWN CALLED ZELIENOPLE

Matt pedals quickly away from school as more and more cars arrive and park. I fly in the road by his side. By now, he can see me whenever he wants to. He doesn't need a slant of light or dust in the air or snowflakes. We're so alike. His cheeks, his chin, his nose are the same as my cheeks, my chin, my nose. Being *here* with him like this, I ache for all the years I missed. But the sound of his breathing, and the way his sparks spray the air, sensing the future he'll have without me, I know it's all heading to a sharp point, an edge, an end.

Soon, no more biking. Soon nothing at all. But for right now, this is everything.

• • •

No one at the station bothers to ask why a schoolkid with a bike is taking a bus. I guess it's easier not to. A bit after nine we jump off at the stop in Zelienople. Matt bikes casually through the streets to the church, me swimming alongside. It's fiercely gray now, and colder than I expect, with no sun and the strong scent of snow on the way. I try to flash forward to how the day might end, but I don't want to press it. Nothing comes anyway.

"We'll start at Macy Tibbs's grave and hope something clicks," I say for probably the third time, just to fill the quiet.

"It better click. It has to click," Matt responds as he has all those times before.

He puts his weight into the pedals, following the map on his phone. He and I learned most things together, walking, talking, playing catch. Some I was better at, some him.

But with biking, we took off equally.

I remember Dad watching us on weekends as we biked around the parking lot of his landscaping company. It was gravel and pebbles and rutted dirt, packed hard by truck and tractor tires, and in the sun of an afternoon, or on a spring dawn before school, Matt and I would go around the lot, one chasing the other, crisscrossing our tracks.

It never got better than that, just wheeling around, and when we bumped and laughed, Dad laughed too; a hard-won laugh, I know now, but a laugh no one's heard for years.

Laughing's over now. The threads twine tighter. The

closer we get to the cemetery, the sooner I'll see birch leaves being buried by snow. The camouflaged man. The shadow in my left eye. The silver that is not a lake. All the final clues will knit together, and that'll be that.

St. Timothy's cemetery is a neat neighborhood of dead folks, a trim garden of stones. The headstones and smaller in-ground plaques for ashes are spread over a wide gentle rise of grass surrounded by a stone wall about waist-high. Some of the upright stones are tilted, others stand straight, an uneven jumble like everything else in this world. The layout of the place reminds me of the streets in Port Haven, but the graveyard is far bigger than we thought it would be.

"Dang," Matt groans. "We need a directory."

Then a question I never thought to ask before wriggles into my mind, and I get a sudden ache in the pit of my stomach. "Do I have one of these?"

Matt leans his bike against the wall. "A gravestone? Of course. In Buckwood."

"Do you ever visit me? I mean, you haven't since I came back, so . . ."

He looks me in the face, then nods. "Dad does. Mom. I always had your bed in my room. That was you to me. Close by. Not in the ground." He turns away.

I wonder what it looks like to see my name, and the dates that go with it. "I'd like to see it before . . . you know, too long."

"Sure, sure." He shivers suddenly and points. "There."

A small house stands on the edge of the lawn against the outer wall. Outside it there's a man in overalls lying next to a tipped-over snow blower, digging at the blades with a kitchen knife.

"Excuse me, sir!" Matt calls.

I expect the guy to shriek, as if one of the yard's inhabitants has decided to visit, but he doesn't flinch. He just jabs at the blades like he's in a knife fight with them. Matt leans and touches the man on his arm.

"Oh holy mother!" the guys shouts. "Where in heaven's name did you come from?" He taps his ear gently with the knife blade. Flecks of rust stick to his lobe. "Didn't hear you!"

Matt smiles. "I'm sorry. I had some—"

"*What?* Marjorie! Marjorie! We have a visitor! And bring my ears!"

A woman totters out of the small house, holding a flower-pot. "Oh good lord!" she says, but not at Matt this time. If her husband can't hear, she can see, and what she sees is me.

"You have a bloody spirit with you!" she gasps.

"What?" the man says. "What's going on?"

Matt sucks in a breath. "My brother, Denis. He died. In fact, we think he was killed near here. We're trying to find out how it happened."

I give her a wave. "Hey."

"What are you looking at?" the man yells at his wife.

She plugs in his hearing aid and hisses into it. "SPEER-IT!"

"Oh? Oh." He squints in my basic direction, then shrugs. "She's got the gift, not me. I got to get this blower working before the snow."

Seriously giving me the eye, his wife says, "What can I help you boys with?"

"Is a man named Macy Tibbs buried here?" Matt asks, and my heart pounds, waiting for the answer.

"Macy Tibbs. Yes, a veteran. Two-thousand-ten." She points toward the far side of the yard. "Row seven, halfway on your left. His son, too, about five years ago."

Matt glances at me. "Which makes sense, with what we know."

Before he can ask anything else, the man butts in, reminding me of someone I used to know. "Tibbs? No one comes to see him anymore, except the other son. Once or twice a year. Not like the fella who visits those *other* graves. He's here all the time."

"Oh, him." His wife sniffs sharply. "I don't like the look of him."

"He's all right," the man says. "I talk to him now and then."

"Who are you talking about?" Matt asks. "What other graves?"

"With the flowers, down there." He points. "His name's Egan. Private First Class, Gary Egan. He's been coming for years. He was here this morning. Always comes on Tuesday."

If a ghost can faint, I'm doing it. "Dad? Is he talking about Dad?"

Matt swings around to me. "Dad wasn't here this morning. It can't possibly—"

"Can be and is. Egan. He showed me his dog tag once. Kind of old to be your dad—"

It takes more time than we'd like for this to click into whatever it's going to click into. We try to work it through, thought after thought, while the man stares at Matt and his wife at me. Then it comes. Matt reaches at my shoulders to shake me.

"It's him!" he says. "Denis, it's the guy who stole your tag! The guy who killed you and laid you at Gettysburg! It's got to be! Excuse me, what graves does he go to?"

But the wife gives out a shriek. "Gettysburg? You're the boy? The poor little boy! Oh, how horrible to die the way you did. Everyone was heartbroken. And your poor dear brother . . ."

It's the first stranger who has spoken of my death, and it stuns me. *"Matt . . . this is what people said to you . . . I'm . . . sorry . . ."*

"Not now." He waves me off. "Where are the graves?"

"There!" The old man points. "Down a bit from the Tibbs's stones. It's a family plot."

"Thank you," Matt says. Together we stalk down the long rows of stones.

We soon find the markers of Macy and Melrose Tibbs, both etched with veteran symbols.

A little farther down, three small cremation stones are set in the cropped grass. We stare at the names and dates. It takes us a moment to realize what we're seeing.

VIRGINIA AGNES MUNRO
MOTHER
OCT 7 1927–DEC 22 2008

RICHARD BYATT MUNRO
SON
SEPT 5 1951–JAN 12 1970

JOSEPH CHESTER EGAN
SON
SEPT 5 1951–NOV 14 2005

I'm breathless and almost choke on the words. "GeeGee. And her twin sons."

"She lived in Zelienople for years," says Matt. "Dad

told me she buried his father's ashes here. They're all here together."

"GeeGee said Richard used her maiden name. She used it too. To honor him, I think."

There is a veteran insignia cut into each son's stone, and sprays of fresh-cut flowers lying aside GeeGee's and Richard's graves, but none at Joseph's.

A sharp icy wind sweeps west over the cemetery. I think of the snow that day five years ago.

Matt draws the cold into his lungs. "So here it is. The missing link between your kidnapping and death, between Maywell Tibbs and your killer, whoever he was. Maybe even that stranger."

I throw that in among my other racing thoughts. "Are we saying that Maywell was at his father's grave, then let me go at the exact moment some guy visited our family's graves? Who in the world was he? And was it just dumb luck that they were both here together exactly then?"

"No, not dumb," Matt says. "Or if it *was* dumb, it was those dumb threads you keep harping about, crossing again and again and weaving together, or some other mumbo jumbo, but here's the thing"—he fixes his eyes on me— "here's the thing, Denis. It was early Tuesday. Maywell was talking to his dead father, and some guy was talking to our people. They both loved people who had died. They loved them. And right in the middle of that ... is you."

It stuns me to hear Matt say this. "Seriously? Love will bring us together? I'm a song!"

Matt looks at me in the cold sunlight. "Except that's what those threads are. However these two guys came together, it was because of what they felt. Now there's just one more thread to follow. This thing is coming together so fast—"

His eyes are suddenly fixed over my shoulder.

"Uh . . . Denis?"

I follow his gaze to where the sky is darkest. There's a ridge of brown hills where the trees have lost their leaves, and then I see it.

I see *it*.

The darker darkness rises.

After five years, that weird looming presence at the edge of my vision turns real and rises high in the far distance, darker than the surrounding darkness.

It's not a tall tree trunk in the hills outside Buckwood. It isn't the drop tower at Funland Amusement Park. It's not an old pine tree at Silver Lake. It isn't the looming granite block of the Georgia State monument at Gettysburg when you kneel beneath it.

It's a massive black chimney. The menacing shadow I see in my mind is a giant brick column, rising like an enormous gravestone over where I died.

And suddenly, I'm running, or not *running*, but floating among the birches, weightless. *I float I drown.* I drift on waves—not real waves—but the rhythmic up and down of being carried, cradled even, in the stranger's arms. The arms of the man who ferries me to my death.

"What's there?" I whisper. "Matt, tell me what's out there?"

He whips out his phone and finds a map. "Remains of a coal mine. The Blue Creek Coal Mine. Holy crow. Could it be a mine our great-grandfather built? Denis, we need to go there."

In my mind I'm already there, frantic and terrified, my living heart bursting inside me, while heavy boots thump the snow-covered ground behind me.

42

CITY OF RUST

The seven miles west to the coal mine are tough going, slow and untraveled. There are hills and rutted, beat-up, sunken roads. The biking is hard, and Matt finds he has to dive into the overgrown roadside weeds whenever I warn him.

"Car!"

"Ahhh!"

In the meantime he doesn't bother to return the two calls and four texts from Mom but manages to leave a weirdly chipper voice mail—"Love you, Mom. Sorry I didn't call at lunch. We had pizza! Call you soon"—hoping there are no birds or airplanes in the background.

The two or three times we pause for him to catch his breath, he reads from his cell phone.

"Blue Creek was a hundred and thirteen years old when it shut down a decade and a half ago. It closed when the market for bituminous coal collapsed."

"I always wondered."

"It's a big complex—steel and concrete and brick, with miles of underground shafts—that nobody can use for anything else. No other industry, I mean. The big brick chimney is part of the original mine. It costs too much to raze the buildings and fill the shafts, so they've just bolted it closed and let it die by itself."

"Shafts? Does that mean anything to us?"

"Not to me. To you?"

I don't know, but it's one of a hurricane of things in my brain. "If someone found me in the cemetery, why on earth bring me out here? Who would do that?"

"The killer. He wanted to kill you."

"So kill me and leave me in the graveyard!"

"He wanted to kill you in private. An abandoned mine is the perfect home for someone who wants to live under the radar. Someone who's hiding out."

Hiding. Yeah. Maybe. Except when he's putting flowers on graves.

It's long past noon by the time we begin to get our first good view of Blue Creek, a sinister, enormous city of steel and brick and stone, rotting in a shallow valley. The sky is dark gray in the west. A white flake zigzags the air in front of my face, and I realize snow has begun to fall. We move on foot among the hangar-size structures and silos, iron sheds, flaking wooden barracks, and rust-pitted tanks. There are lifts, octopus chains with massive hooks, overturned shuttle cars, rusting winches, wheels, drums, engines, complex pulleys and cables, conduits, beams, fans, chutes, and mazes of crisscrossing metal stairways strung up to the peaked roofs and highest reaches of the dead city. Towering above this wrecked terrain, visible from every angle, like the old coaster at Funland, the great brick chimney rises, a dead beacon.

It's a stage set for the end of the world.

My throat tightens. My chest sinks. *I float I drown.* Of course I do. The killer is carrying me through the frozen leaves, over the rail tracks, between the ghostly trunks, while each falling snowflake says this is where I died five years ago.

A coal mine in a valley west of Zelienople on the Tuesday before Thanksgiving.

Am I here now with Matt, or am I five years ago on the day I died?

Or am I seeing, being, doing, living both at once?

"What do you remember?" he whispers.

Three giant conduits slant up from the mine's mouths to

the buildings where the coal is prepared. The nearest one is angled like a fallen column, its windows smashed like broken teeth.

"I was so cold and starved, I was probably dying already, hallucinating my brain out."

I sense Matt imagining his seven-year-old brother, wounded and lost, being carried into this defunct factory. "This place . . . this place . . . Denis, I'm . . ."

I get it. We're both sorry. There are no words.

If snowflakes collect on black cinders like tiny wet diamonds, everything else is gunmetal gray. A massive slant-roofed structure stands to our left. In it hangs a rusted door. Of all the barred and chained and welded doors in sight, this door alone stands open.

Matt watches the flakes fill me. "Why is that the only door open?"

"Because he's still here," I whisper. The dark opening, with now and then a white flake crossing to the ground, draws me to it. Matt tries the door gently with both hands. It squeals like the hunger-cry of a hawk. I touch his arm and he stops. "Can you slip inside? I know I can."

He draws in a breath. He nods. We enter together.

It is scarcely warmer inside. Everything is prickled with a fur of frost. It reminds me of the cold iron shed of the razor. As in that painful room, there is a human smell inside these walls.

I sense Matt's terror, but also his bravery. He's my brother, and he's doing this for real. He's feeling real iron, real coldness, real fright, real danger. Sure, I have something to lose, but never as much as him, not if there's a killer here, and there is, I sense it.

We're mere minutes from meeting . . . him. I sense that too.

Matt tugs out his phone, opens the flashlight. "Eighteen percent battery. No service."

Some dozen feet along a narrow corridor, we enter an office, perhaps, or a small workshop. A string of inside windows, smeared with soot, looks out over an open area below. A high wooden bench in front is heaped with trash, the remains of food, bowls smudged with the muck of some old meal that reeks.

"This guy is in for the long haul." Matt nods with his chin. "Look at all this junk."

Stacks of batteries, certainly over a hundred, are piled on the bench next to several sizes of flashlights. There are three portable radios and a rusted camp stove with four canisters of propane. A pile of newspapers stands arched against the wall, almost to the ceiling.

Lying open facedown on the workbench is a dusty book. Matt picks it up. *American Battlefields*. Maps are pinned to the wall. Pennsylvania. Georgia. Vietnam.

"Holy whoa and a half. Look at this." Underneath the

book, Matt finds a brittle newspaper, oil-stained and yellow as mustard. The headline shouts:

BUCKWOOD BOY MISSING SINCE SUNDAY

Matt reads the familiar article. "This was published on Monday before they found you. That means he already knew who you were when he saw you in the cemetery!"

"He knew I was missing. He went to the cemetery like he always did. But that day was different. Maybe he heard Maywell Tibbs screech away in Jenny. However it happened, he found a boy lying in the snow. He ran over, read the dog tag, and knew I was the missing boy."

"And because he was nuts or couldn't let on where he was or whatever, the killer brought you here. Denis, we've searched enough. We have evidence. We need to get the police—"

Killer? Yes, but . . . there's more. "I need to keep looking, Matt. With or without you."

"I sure as heck am not leaving you here."

"Need me, don't you? Admit it."

He doesn't. It's then that I see the torn clipping pinned to the wall over the workbench, like a cross over an altar. It's faded and curled, so there's no reading it, but I see the photo.

A child's face. Not mine. My heart stops. "Matt? Holy crow, Matt—"

Something clanks down the corridor. Footsteps scratch the floor.

Matt instantly flicks off his light. His eyes glisten in the gray room. A shadow moves jerkily across the door light—just like it did when I was in the crib at GeeGee's house.

Matt quickly wedges himself up against the row of steel lockers. He is still clutching the newspaper. I hover beside him. The man enters the room, moving swiftly around the workbench in the dark. He knows where things are, takes up a flashlight, beaming it around the room, where it shines back from the black window, reflecting his face darkly.

And my heart stops again. "I . . . I . . . I *know him!*"

"Watt?"

The man freezes.

A low growl roars up inside of him, shaking the room with its rolling thunder. The newspaper is gone. Someone's been messing with his stuff. He tears an angry look around. Matt is crouched and invisible, but now I see the face clearly. And yes, I know him. I know him, and suddenly, it strikes me like a barrage of gunfire. Every nerve in my body sparks and burns.

"*Matt, it's Dad's father! That man is Joseph Egan!*"

I try to whisper this in my head, but it comes out like a scream, and the man jerks backward, as if he heard me speak his name. He staggers from the workshop, tramps quickly through the rooms, one arm flailing high in the air. I fly outside just in time to see the man I know is Dad's father stumble between the broken buildings, jerking through the jagged yellow leaves and vanishing in the trees.

Matt runs to me, breathless. "What the heck are you saying? Dad's father is dead!"

"Except he isn't. He couldn't be. I know that face. It's him. It has to be."

"How do you know his face? Mom destroyed all his pictures—"

"It all fits! Dad was in the hospital or jail when his father 'died,' which he only knew because GeeGee told him. He knew he was buried up here, but that was all."

"You're nuts. You can't possibly know what he looks like."

"I know that face! There's nothing under his gravestone, there can't be!"

Even as our grandfather runs farther and farther away, I read his fear, spitting sparks that slash the air. He was shattered from the bus crash, his leg gone. But even after he'd hurt everyone, GeeGee had pity on her son. She gave him a grave marker and helped him go away.

"All he wanted was to be no one, living alone," I say. "And until I blundered into his world, he was alone. Except for when he was watching over us. When Dad was away, his father watched us. He knew something was wrong at Gee-Gee's that day. The house was dark, the phone rang and rang unanswered. He was the man who picked me up, the day I cut my eyebrow, the day GeeGee died. Mom didn't recognize him because she was sure he was dead."

Matt's eyes flick back and forth, trying to understand it. "That's . . . insane."

"He knew when I was missing. That Tuesday, he was at the cemetery as he always was, visiting GeeGee's and his brother's graves. When he saw me, he knew me, and he carried me here, floated me above the ground in his arms."

I float I drown.

Lost and terrified, dying of cold and hunger, I had accidentally mysteriously miraculously been dropped on his doorstep, and he ferried me to his home. Broken in two because of the girl's death, he might have sensed in me the peace that could be his if only he saved me.

Snow is falling heavily now. Dad's father has run away. He will hide again and lose himself one more time. I want to go after him, finish this mystery once and for all, but I'm torn from my thoughts by a sudden crush of leaves.

The sound comes not from the snowy woods where Joseph is fleeing.

It comes from behind us.

43

KILLER

"Matt! *Matt!*"

Our dad shouts over and over as he hurries toward us, Mom at his side, fuming and crying. Trey scrambles behind through the drifting flakes, Trey's mouth hanging open, Trey's cheeks red, lips red, eyes red with fright. Four police officers tramp quickly after them, but stand back and fan out as Mom rushes to Matt first.

"My God, Matt! What in heaven's name are you doing here? You lied! Forcing Trey to cover for you! How could you do that to us? All alone here? You could have been killed—"

"Mom, Dad, no, I'm with Denis," he says, and Trey smiles faintly, trying to find me in the gray light. I love Trey, I love Trey being here.

Dad grits his teeth. "You're *not* with Denis! Stop that—"

"I *am* with him, he's right here, and we're finding things. We're close to where Denis died, I know it. *Denis* knows it! Dad, it's your father. He's the killer—"

"Joseph Egan didn't kill me," I say, without knowing why, but Matt can't seem to hear my words. The noise in his head is too loud and he repeats it.

"Mom, Dad, he's the killer and he's here and he's alive!"

Mom is livid, raises her hand, but Dad steps in front of her. "Matt, cut it out! What are you talking about? You know what, never mind. Just come with us—"

"Dad, no!" Matt wriggles away and trembles like the yellow leaves drifting over the rails. "Your father's here. Our *grandfather.* Joseph Egan. He murdered Denis! He's the killer."

Now that I finally know who it is, the word *killer* bites in my mind with an even icier sharpness. GeeGee's words shoot back to me like an arrow in the chest. I repeat them to Matt.

"GeeGee said, he was wrong, he was sorry. I think she meant that Joseph had changed—"

"Matt, come on," Mom gasps. "Joseph Egan is buried a few miles from here. We can show you—"

"That grave is empty. It has to be! Dad, your father came to GeeGee's house when you were in Valdosta. He was watching us. Watching *over* us. GeeGee helped him run away after the bus accident. He changed after the girl was killed. Whatever he did, we think he went away and finally hid here, to be close to the graves of his mother and brother."

"Matt, you're not making any sense," Dad says, and two of the police officers step forward. "That was some random stalker," he adds, glancing at Mom. "Your mother told me. I know that now."

"He's right, Mr. and Mrs. Egan, about it all," Trey says firmly. "Denis is here, really. I can almost see him." And Trey points to exactly where I stand. Matt tries, but sees only snow. "I've worked on this with Matt, and Denis too, all of it, backward from Gettysburg to here."

Shaking his head, Dad wipes the heavy wet flakes from his cheeks. "This is over. We're going home. Everyone."

"Wait," says Mom. Sucking in a great big breath to swear or scream in frustration, she simply holds it, holds it, and lets it out. "I want to hear. Tell me, Matt. Tell *us*. Right now."

It's amazing that the police are saying nothing, but simply wait for this to end, like Matt's good teacher waited. Snow is slashing hard at the buildings now. I hear each flake slice like a knife blade. I feel every heartbeat. The air is alive with motion and sound and smell and touch.

"Our grandfather wasn't killed by the bus," Matt says, getting control of himself. "He lost his leg, yeah. Dad, you think he died because GeeGee—your grandmother—told you he did. But he must have changed in the hospital. Maybe because the girl died. Anyway, GeeGee let him get away. She forgave him, but you never would. Denis told me she visited you and tried to tell you. Last year. Ghosts can do that. They can visit you."

Dad stands, head lowered, eyes closed, listening.

"So he goes underground," says Trey. "Off the grid. Everybody loses track of him. He has no one, anymore, so he just disappears."

Matt nods repeatedly. "It's so easy, it's so easy, to drift away, and that's what he did. He hides here. We saw him, Dad. We *saw* him just now. Plus look what we found in that building."

Matt hands Dad the newspaper. He takes it in his quivering hands. "What about it?"

"He had this. He knew Denis was missing. And, Mom, when we were at GeeGee's house, he was watching. He saw it wasn't right. No lights. Denis crying. The phone ringing off the hook. That's why he broke in."

Mom listens to him, the police listen. One of the officers says it's fantastic, a nightmare. Another calls the local station. I hear the words, "Check this out."

"You came up with all of this?" Dad says.

Matt looks at Trey, then at him. "We all did."

"But why did he . . . Why would your grandfather hurt Denis?" Mom asks. "Why leave clues for someone to solve the murder he committed? It doesn't make sense."

"Because it wasn't murder!"

I yell this, but Matt can't hear. More police cars roar up

the road to the mine. More sirens sound from behind the buildings. They are surrounding the mine complex.

"The reason he killed Denis," Matt adds, "must go back years. Denis is always on about threads connecting things. Maybe it's something from long ago. Denis doesn't get it, either."

He looks for me, not where I am.

"Matt, can you hear me?" I ask. He can't, not a word.

"Matt, I'm sorry. I really can't believe any of this . . . ," Mom says, but in a whisper. She's confused, and shedding angry sparks like at the Silver Lake Lodge that day.

From inside the building comes a sound of clanking.

Dad jerks around. "What on earth?"

Joseph came back? Why would he come back? He'd fled into the woods. Vanished. Gone again. Why return? Have the police encircled the mine, trapping him? Did he come back because we're here? His family? Does he even know who is here?

A walkie-talkie crackles, and the officers with us spring into action, flanking the open door, while I fly straight through.

"Stand back!" an officer commands, but Matt jumps inside after me.

"Matt, get out of there!" Trey yells from outside.

Guns drawn, two officers move into the doorway when a metal pipe flies down the corridor. One officer ducks, the other falls back on her heels outside the door. The door is kicked shut. Joseph whirls around, stumbles past me, half slides down the metal stairs to the workshop below.

"*Joseph, stop!*" I cry, but he doesn't stop. He can't hear me, either.

The door flies open, and Dad is there. Four cops push in ahead.

Trey calls, "Matt, get back here!"

But Matt has run after the man. Footsteps thunder across the empty room below. As I fly down to it, metal squeals horribly. There's a rush of cold. Joseph has run back outside. I don't see Matt anywhere. I rush outside too, chasing a whirl of snowflakes from the rear of the building through the frozen leaves. The officers all have their weapons out, shouting.

44

THE ASHES OF JOSEPH EGAN

The old man lurches among the abandoned structures, the rusted rails. I hear his footsteps, thumping awkwardly over the wooden ties through the tall weeds. I follow.

"Granddad, wait!"

Does he sense me? I have to think he does. Like you "see" the heat signatures of living things in a nighttime scope. But his weave of emotions and thoughts is so heavy and intricate. This is the revelation he knew would come, the capture he must have feared.

Matt scurries behind the coal crusher, Trey screaming at him to stop, both of them outpacing Mom and Dad. Snow falls heavily as Joseph arcs through the trees fringing the buildings, drawing the cops into the woods after him. But he cuts sharply back to an alley of railcars behind the black-ened chimney. He's rounding the chimney like some kind of totem, then bolts away between the buildings. And there is Matt.

Suddenly, it's five years ago as Joseph wheels around in the gathering snow. I'm reliving that day *and* today. Joseph and Matt move the way Joseph and I did. Time repeats itself.

Matt races down an opening between high-walled win-dowless buildings under the conveyor. I fly after him—*"Matt, no!"*—but I'm sluggish, heavy. The police number eight or ten now, but are surrounding the wrong structures. I'm stupidly helpless, unable to call to them. Matt barrels out of the alley into a honeycomb of corrugated sheds. Nothing I do is fast enough. I have no more power than a breath.

"Matt, stop running!" I yell, but he doesn't, instead tears blindly past the coal silos, the tanks. Thinking fast, thinking wrong, he follows the rails toward the mine shafts.

Joseph is suddenly there. He grabs Matt by the arm, twists him around, and in that instant is shocked to see my face in Matt's. Dad's other tag hangs around Matt's neck, and he knows now what we know. He cries a word that may not even be a word.

Matt struggles in his grasp. "You killed my brother! Your own grandson! Police! Over here!" He wriggles away and stumbles toward a rusted door.

"No! No!" the old man grunts.

I remember that door. It leads to a shaft. I fly through before Matt reaches it. I look down into the abyss. In his panic, Matt cannot light up his phone.

"Matt, stop. There's a mine shaft here!"

He still can't hear me, as I can't help remembering that day five years ago.

I stumbled through that door, terrified of the monster chasing me. I tripped into the darkness of the chamber, hurt, confused, soaked. His face was suddenly there, the face I didn't know then, leaning over me, black eyes drilling into me, the toothless mouth grunting.

"I'm your grggg— I'm your grrr—"

He tried to say he knew me. I would not hear, like Matt can't hear now. I ran from him. Stupidly I ran. I ran from my grandfather. He lurched after me, calling what only now I understand. "Not there!"

He threw himself at me, howling, and clamped his hand on my foot to hold me fast. I wriggled away, losing my shoe. I snatched it up and ran on cinders, cutting my foot. As I ran then, Matt runs now. I tripped. I fell. Matt trips and falls. I screamed. Matt screams.

I pulled away from the old man's grasping hands. His pants were in shreds, from his shoe to his thigh, a construction of rods and hinges, his prosthetic leg.

There is silver.

I pulled away and dropped headlong into the slope shaft, breaking myself, crushing my neck, my eyes recording the last thing I saw, flashing like the surface of the moonlit lake, like five years ago in Port Haven, when I cried out—*"Silver leg! Silver leg!"*

Joseph gave out an animal cry when I plummeted. Frantic, he must have crawled after me to the bottom. He saw his grandson dead. The sobbing grandson he had soothed five years before. Was he the cause of this child's death? He'd watched over my brother and me for years, but I had died. Just like the girl had died. This time, he tried to stop it. But I died anyway.

"Mommy!" Matt cries, held by the old man's hands at the lip of the shaft. Joseph tries to pull Matt clear, but loses his grip. Matt scuffles back, identical to the way I did, to the lip of the shaft.

"Matt, no! Let him help you!"

And without thinking, I leap at Matt myself. I slam him hard and hold him tight, when all at once, our father bursts in, shocked to see *his* father alive.

Joseph turns his startled face. His dark eyes widen. He teeters on the edge before his living foot gives way. Their hands miss each other. He disappears down the shaft. There is a sickening thump.

"Matt!" Trey cries out, pushing into the opening. "I

thought I lost you!" The two wrap themselves in each other's arms, Matt in Trey's, and Trey in his, and they are one person.

Three officers burrow into the chamber now, with Mom behind, their flashlights glinting down the shaft. Joseph Egan is twisted impossibly at the bottom. Next to him, half-covered in dust and ash, is my sneaker. Later, I think, if they look hard enough, they'll find my missing tooth.

Ignoring the officers, Dad struggles down the long slope of the shaft. He heaves his father's limp body onto his shoulders and climbs it back up. The weight on his back, the heaviness he's carried for years, is finally real.

Exhausted, Dad lays the body at the mouth of the shaft while Mom holds Matt and Trey together. The suffering man who watched over my brother and me is dead. Mom coughs out sob after sob. The police are everywhere and help Dad carry the body out through the driving snow.

Gazing on that crusty face, a face I've never seen before but know so well, I understand for certain what had nagged me, scratched at me for so long. My murder wasn't murder.

It was never murder.

It was an accident.

But accident or not, Joseph Egan is dead now too.

45

FLIGHTS OF ANGELS

After more interrogations than I can count, streams of odd explanations, reports, all the flimsy brutal overwhelming nonsensical wisps of evidence that Matt and Trey—and Mom and Dad—reconstructed, we were home in Buckwood once more.

Not long after, we heard that Momma-May Tibbs passed away. Another sorrow in November. Maywell was soon arrested and confessed to his strange part in my murder.

End of story.

Sort of.

I should have gone back to Port Haven and GeeGee right then, I should have. But I was held here. By a thread, maybe, but a thread nearly impossible to break.

•   •   •

"Can you imagine?" Matt says a few nights later in his room. "A one-legged man—*an old and battered one-legged man*—making his way all the way to the bottom of a mine shaft to get you. And then to bring you back up? It's tough on regular people. It was tough on Dad. But with one leg?"

I imagine the scene in that shaft.

Weeping, Joseph hoisted me onto his back; weeping, he hauled me to the top. Weeping, he laid me on the cot in the room where he made his home. He cleaned me up, he stole aboard the train and boosted an old Honda from a parking lot, easy for someone who had foraged for years. He lowered me into its back seat and drove and drove, at first not knowing where to go.

And then he remembers things. Georgia. How our dad studied the Civil War. The portrait of Byatt at GeeGee's house. The name Byatt on his brother's gravestone. Who knows how many threads drew him to Gettysburg and the Georgia monument. Once there, he pulled Dad's tag from my neck when he placed me at the monument. No, that's not right. He gently slipped the dog tag over my head and placed me at the monument, my cheek resting against the cool stone.

If my dad ever understood the clues, he'd know that what happened to me was an accident. That Joseph was innocent. He was wrong, he was sorry. He was just doing his poor human best.

"He loved our family," Matt says to me. "He loved the two of us, finally."

"It's probably way more complicated than that."

But even complicated, it all wove together, and made perfect, painful sense.

"The whole Tibbs family means something," I say. "Without Maywell at his father's grave, Dad's father might never have seen me. Without that, we'd never know he was alive."

Matt looks at me sadly. "I guess in a crazy way, those two bad brothers gave us back our family. Dad got his father back, for a few minutes, anyway. They cleared up the secrets. That's a lot—" His phone bings. He reads the screen and smiles. "Trey's coming over."

In Matt's room are his single bed, new computer, books, everything that he's gotten because I died, but they're nothing at all, compared to the real prize.

"I love it when Trey's around," I tell him.

"I'm pretty sure it's mutual."

Matt once called me lucky. He was right. I'm mainly lucky that he remembered me with so much love. He brought me back. He kept me here and gave me a home again, for a little while.

"I'll leave you two for a bit," I tell him. "I have to settle a couple of things up there."

"It'll hurt, won't it?" Matt asks. "Sorry, I know it will. But don't be long."

"From you, bro? Never."

But *never* is the wrong word. It's not really one I should use about anything. I'll come back to Matt, sure, but I know I can't stay. It's not right to hang around when others need the space.

Like somebody told me once, holding on to a person might simply be holding him back.

Besides, we'll all meet again somewhere, sometime, yes?

I return to Port Haven and walk down to the shore to see the big boats coming in. It hurts to be sliced, of course, but whatever. I'd already worked out that today will be a special day. On the beach, I see two baseball-capped men tossing a softball back and forth. Melrose and his father, probably waiting for Momma-May to arrive.

The writer . . . Russell, I remember . . . is sitting on the porch of the beach club with GeeGee, who is quiet but smiling. I guess living at my house agrees with her. The kid with the itchy back is gone. So is the grouchy lady in sunglasses. Their stories are over.

Russell fingers his notebook, but doesn't focus on it, just lets it move in his hands until it slips away from him and lies closed on the table. His hair is so thin I see his skin beneath the strands.

He smiles a half smile. "I can't read my own words any-more, D . . ."

"Denis."

"The words are pulling away from me." He lays his hands one over the other on the tabletop. They remind me of the way hands are placed in a coffin. "But maybe you can make something beautiful. Take it." He pushes his notebook to me.

"No, Russell. That's your whole life."

"There are plenty of blank pages left." He looks up toward the blue hills to the north. "It's time for me to go. But I think, I think"—he smiles a smile of such warmth that I myself am torn between smiling or crying—"I think, you'll be a poet for us, yes? Write the stories I never could. I think that would be wonderful. You learned so much down there. There's a lot to be said for having been a mingler. Go on. Take it, please."

GeeGee nods at me, as if she understands what's hap-pening. I place my hand on Russell's shoulder, as thin and insubstantial as hers. "Thanks, Russell."

I open the notebook to the folded page and read his words about me.

It snowed at Silver Lake the day I died.

"May I?" I take his pen and add a second line.

BUT THAT'S NOT WHERE I DIED.

Which seems to end it as well as anything.

All at once I hear a big cheer go up. Feet stomp the board-walk that leads to the piers. I've been waiting for this. I hop down and search the crowd for Pink Hair. I find him waving to the thick crowd of arrivals bending at the railing of a giant ocean liner.

I run down to join him. I nudge his arm. "Hello, Uncle Richard. Well, great-uncle."

He turns, frowns, then grins. "What do you know? I *thought* you looked familiar! I guess being a mingler ain't the end of the world, after all."

I point to the stern of the ship. "Your brother's up there. I know what he looks like because of you. See him?"

Uncle Richard scans the railing, and there is his brother, Joseph, smiling down at us, the wiry old man who died saving Matt. The man whose face I saw for the first time at the mine yet knew I'd been seeing for years, on his twin brother. Pink Hair. Richard Byatt Munro.

Joseph raises his hand, gives his brother a sign. Pink Hair blows him a kiss. I wave to my grandfather, too, then watch him search the crowd. Turning, I see Gabby. The girl we call Ellen or Ella, but whose name most likely is Gabriella. The girl who died in the bus accident in Valdosta, the girl whose photo was pinned on Joseph's wall at the coal mine, the girl who was remembered from the day she died and kept seven years and ten months old all these years.

Gabby waves to Joseph too. It's like that here. One of the very best things about getting pure is losing the anger you might have learned in life. It's a pretty good feeling.

More cheers float across the dock, as the passengers rush down the gangplank to us.

How long my grandfather will stay in Port Haven, I don't know.

There's Matt and Trey and Mom and Dad to remember him, of course, and maybe that'll be enough for a while. I'll find him later and tell him what he's missed, as much as I remember.

Me? I'll visit Matt for a little while, then I'll stop visiting and look from the grotto, then I'll stop doing that, too. They'll cope. More than cope, they'll move on. There's so much for them down there, and not enough for me.

And I'll see them eventually, anyway, right? Like Uncle Richard waited for his brother for years, I'll wait for Matt. I'll try. And I'll keep GeeGee here for as long as I can, too. I don't know, of course, how soon I'll really start to fade. I could be in Port Haven for a while yet. I mean, what if Matt grows up and names one of his kids after me and explains all about me?

That would be cool.

It seems like the least he can do.

46

ONE LAST THING

A thousand, thousand threads! Patterns woven and repeated, subtly or accidentally, over the years. One thing I've figured out, though. Those threads aren't just lines connecting and reconnecting. They're more like arteries, pumping life from one thing to another, creating not simply patterns in a fabric, but a living connection from person to place to thing. I like that I know this. Of course, one of those living patterns is how, after everything that's happened, after all the secrets they no longer have, Dad and Mom decide to tough it out.

Sure, Dad's coming to terms with who his father really was and who he became at the end, but the ghosts that haunted Dad for years are finally at peace. He's put his father's picture back on the mantel, along with Richard's, GeeGee's, and the crinkly silver one of her grandfather Byatt, posing in his uniform. Some bunch, huh?

And Mom?

She'll have to untangle the whole business about the man Dad fought and who she thought died because of what she'd said, who later picked me up and stopped my crying, who tried to save me and failed, who then saved Matt and died. What a weave that is!

It's not going to be easy for either of them. They still have lots of silences between them, junk that darkens the room, even when Matt's there with them. So far that's kept them from seeing and hearing any trace of me.

Still, they're beginning to feel something sparkly moving between each other that wasn't there before. I guess I can take credit for a little of that. The light's not always there, but when it is, it's blue and yellow and even a kind of pale gold. Maybe sparks are part of the weave, too—opposite colors that make a surprising new pattern. Maybe they'll make something beautiful with them. Only living people can.

For Matt, I have to believe he and Trey are going in a whole different direction, their own. Maybe I'll hear about it someday, if I'm still here.

One evening at supper, a week or so after Zelienople, I'm aching over how to leave them all, when Matt tells our parents completely out of the blue that I'm at the table with them.

"He's standing right here, and he loves us."

After all that's happened, Mom and Dad think they understand, but they don't believe in me that way, and that's okay for now.

"Denis," he says to me in front of them, "you gotta say something or do something so they believe. I know you can."

They search not where I'm standing but Matt's face. They're half hopeful, half worried about him, but without any trace of disapproval. If Matt wants to believe in me, maybe it's all right that he does. This is all said silently between them, with their eyes, and I sense light coming into them as it never has. The zinging at the table pops like a little firework display.

"Denis brought me through this." Matt turns to me. "You did, Denis."

"Somebody had to."

"Come on. Show them. Please."

"Let me think of something. Hold the fort."

"Hold your own farts," Matt snaps, then he relaxes. "Okay, so never mind tonight. Maybe later. He's not magic. Just a ghost."

A minute later he asks, "Mom, do you think we can put Denis's chair back out? So he can sit?"

I look to see if Mom reacts as she has in the past, with big gray defensive shields going up. But there's none of that here.

"I guess so. Wouldn't want him to have to stand all day."

Matt smiles. "Cool."

Mom hugs him tight and long. When he's free, he turns to Dad. Apparently, this is a night of meaningful words, a big deal for Matt, but he's working it.

"Dad . . . I want to thank you."

"Me? For what?"

"For coming from that place you did, and being different. You were. You love us, I know you do. You didn't grow up in a great place, but you're a good man—" He suddenly puts his face on Dad's shoulder and breaks down. My face streams with tears too.

"I love you, Matt. I love you, I love you!" Dad is all over him, wrapping him tight and keeping him there for minutes.

A few days later I do think of a thing. Maybe one of my very last things, after all.

Matt's been quiet and attentive in school. He's thoughtful at home, not cranky or sullen with Mom or Dad. He helps with stuff, and he's present when he needs to be. He's at peace with himself. As much as a twelve-year-old with a serious crush can be at peace. For me, aside from the occasional jokey haunt, I've been hanging off, not interfering, just watching. Matt seems fine with that. He knows I'm not far away.

Then a moment comes.

After that early snow across the state, the temperature climbed, and though the leaves are long down, the air is crisp and the sun stretching low across the yards. Then late one afternoon, without anyone saying much, like a troupe of players getting ready to go onstage, first Dad, then Mom, and finally Matt hop quietly into the car.

I breeze in next to him. *"Where we going?"*

Matt smiles a flat smile. *"Road trip. You'll pee."*

"I hope that means 'I'll see.'"

He gives me a grin that tells me he knows exactly what he's saying and probably has for a while.

Mom drives to the corner, says a few words to Dad, but nobody's really talking, just looking out the windows at the neighborhoods in the last of the light before cold settles in. Dad's the first to mention that this is the first time they've been in the car together, just them, for weeks.

"It is," Mom agrees. "Wow. It's nice."

Matt recalls things we used to do together as a family, and I sense him thinking about that game he and I used to play in the back seat on long drives, the same spelling game he and Trey played on the way to Silver Lake. I think I'll probably be gone before either of us remember what it's called. But that's okay. I love being in the back with him, our parents in front, all of us being quiet. It's that way for a few miles, when Mom slows down and stops the car.

I look out my window at a scattering of small upright stones on a hillside.

I turn to Matt for an explanation.

"It's today," he says, and I realize it's Tuesday before Thanksgiving. Somewhere far away in my mind, I hear Gee-Gee saying *Five years,* in that musical voice I need to hear more of.

We get out together and walk up the brown grass. I'm suddenly filled with something as clear and invisible as it is heavy and dense. My throat thickens, and I want to cry.

We've stopped at a small stone. Simple. No extra words.

DENIS RICHARD EGAN
SEPT 14 2006–NOV 20 2013

The marker is mine and not mine. I see my name graven into the stone and want to trace my fingers in it, like Dad did the stone at Gettysburg, but I know it's just a signpost, and not where I am, a road sign with an arrow, telling people to look for me in another place.

"Nice," I whisper to Matt, trying not to choke on my tears. "*Thank them for me.*"

I know there isn't much time left. I have to get back. It's where I belong. But looking at Matt now, his crumpled face, his eyes red and wet, I only want to make him laugh. I only want to remember his smiling face forever.

Then, all at once, the name of that old back seat road game pops into my mind. I'm about to tell him when Mom gasps through her tears.

"Oh, the light is so perfect on the stone. I want a picture of all my boys. Stand on each side of Denis. You look so handsome!"

A photograph? Thank you, Mom!

Matt and Dad turn and lean their heads close over the stone, and when I squirrel between them, Dad moves a little away, as if to make room. For what, he's not sure.

I choose my moment. With orange light streaming over her shoulder and out of her fingers, Mom taps her phone and I shout in Matt's head, for one of the last times.

"*Montezuma!*"

"That's it!" he cries as snot bursts from his nose.

Mom groans. "Oh, Matt! You ruined it. Your face!"

But when she taps her phone to see the photo, she lets out a cry. "Oh . . . oh, look! Gary, look!"

And there I am, amid a shower of golden sparks—my own handsome face, laughing between Dad and Matt, my brother, my twin forever.

Egan Family Tree

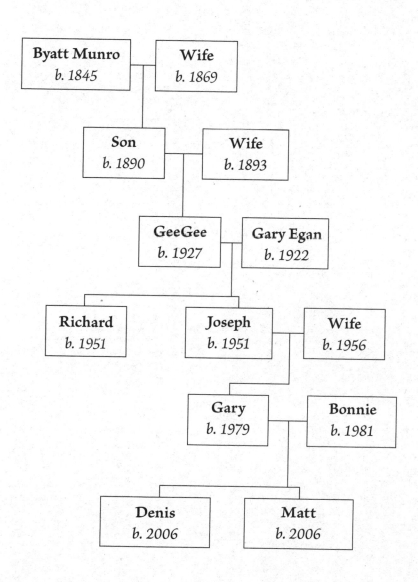

ACKNOWLEDGMENTS

From the original one-sentence idea that spent some time kicking around in my brain, this story has evolved into something quite unexpected and thrilling. I want to thank my editor, Claudia Gabel, for seeing in that first gauzy notion a unique way forward. To all my friends at Katherine Tegen Books, my gratitude for being part of the ongoing fun of creating books for young readers. As always, to my children and my wife I owe countless loving debts, for simply being you, and for allowing me the space and time and calm to keep doing what I so love.

One other, probably very minor thing. Readers will likely not consider important the short bit about sidewalks in chapter 11, but the mere mention of the word means a lot to a person of a certain age for whom that concrete river along our yards was not just a cracked place to run and sit and play, but a thoroughfare leading, left or right, to the huge reckless world beyond. Reading those couple of sentences during my last pass at these pages, I was reminded of the great homage to sidewalks in the opening of Bruce Brooks's brilliant *Everywhere*. And here is the power of writing from the heart: I've realized I can't separate, nor do I ever want to, neighborhood sidewalks from Bruce's words. He has *done* them. The music of his attention to them is there, and will continue to be there, in every sidewalk I write and in every sidewalk I use. To me, this is the indissoluble bond between writing and the world we live in.